THE GUARDIAN INITIATIVE

PREQUEL TO THE ELIOUD LEGACY SERIES

LIANE ZANE

ZEPHON ROMANCE
BOSTON, MASSACHUSETTS

Digital Edition AUGUST 2024 ISBN: 978-1-963515-07-7

Print Edition ISBN: 978-1-963515-08-4

Cover design by Betelgeuse, 99Designs

To my guardian angel

ONE

If dawn was anything to go by, it was going to be a glorious day. Then again, thought Olivia Markham, nearly every day in Kotor had turned out to be glorious, even in rainy winter when the temperature averaged in the mid-40s. Anyone who grew up outside of Boston knew that New Englanders called that shorts weather.

She smiled to herself at the thought as she stretched out before her daily hike. It really was a smile, though she felt the tinge of sadness that caught in her chest. She hadn't been home for Christmas in two years.

Today, in early June, the temperature in this coastal city along the eastern Adriatic would peak in the low 80s. But right now, at 5 a.m., the temperature hovered around 60—plenty warm when hiking up the Ladder to the ruins of the fortress. Olivia hiked this section of the Ladder daily, pushing herself to complete the two-and-a-half-kilometer loop in 30 minutes. It wasn't exactly a day at the Farm or even a day training embedded with a Special Tactical Unit at the CIA, but she did her best to challenge herself. She often added a weighted pack, for instance, or forced herself to do it twice back-to-back.

This morning, she wore wicking workout clothing and an innovative lightweight shoe described as a 'foot glove,' with a flexible sole and individual toes. Invented by a Massachusetts company, the unique footwear imitated the bare feet of primitive runners and certain modern-day people in remote regions of the world. Her father had sent them to her for Christmas. She'd only just gotten them from whomever in Prague, her last posting, forwarded her mail and packages. Somehow her father always managed to give her just the right gift at the right time, even when he had no idea where she lived or what she did. She had extended leave due, and she intended to thank him in person.

"Right, time to stop stalling, Olivia," she said, looking up the trail. She'd already sprinted the four-hundred-fifty meters from her apartment on St. Tryphon's Square. She was plenty warmed up.

Trouble was, she'd been trying to conquer this length of trail in these 'innovative' shoes all week—at least, without twisting her ankle, which she'd already hidden from Étienne. Thankfully, the bruises from her spectacular fall on day one had healed before he'd seen her in the shower.

In the low light of dawn, the rocky trailhead on Tabaćina Street didn't look promising. She'd left the picturesque Old Town, and several low concrete buildings squatted alongside the road.

Though serious hikers knew about the Ladder, most tourists chose to climb up to the Castle of San Giovanni along the crumbling Walls of Kotor. Olivia saw them daily taking the official southern entrance near her apartment. The Ladder, on the other hand, was best hiked in early morning or late afternoon when it was cooler. Not periods when most tourists disembarked from their cruise ships.

Olivia looked up toward the mountains above the coast. The Ladder, whose seventy-plus switchbacks and quickly rising elevation had been the only route for centuries to Cetinje, the former royal capital, zigzagged up the steep slope. Poor souls had traversed its entire six-and-a-half kilometers in archaic dress, even sometimes in winter when the snow had to be painstakingly cleared. No wonder they situated a chapel halfway up. It must have served as an aid station in more than one sense.

If she could do this easier section without falling, she'd conquer the whole damn rocky trail in these alien foot gloves.

Olivia set out at a brisk pace, her lightweight pack with its water bottle and protein bar not yet heavy on her back. The rising sun warmed her skin as she picked her way around each sharp turn, but she was rewarded with views of the bay and the red-roofed buildings of Old Town cradled by the mountainous shore. They never ceased to fill her with awe and a sense of gratitude. It was good to be alive.

Perhaps she shared that feeling with those earlier hikers, that reward for their toil.

And then, despite knowing better, Olivia fell into a kind of trance at the monotonous doubling back every 30 meters.

On the third acute turn, as she looked toward Kotor searching for a glimpse of St. Tryphon Cathedral, her right foot slid on a smooth stone half buried in the uneven terrain, twisting her foot before she caught herself. Her heart lurched. Thankfully, she hadn't wrenched her ankle.

Olivia touched a fingertip to the small pendant on her chest and continued on, focusing on her breath and imagining that her bare soles felt every stone along the uneven ground. She'd forgotten this technique of mastering a challenge, the power of visualization, of seeing herself succeed. *Sensei* Mark used to say that faith was just imagination in practice.

Ten minutes later, Olivia stopped at the small Chapel of St. John long enough to drink water and eat a protein bar in quick, neat bites. She could have eaten it along the trail, but she didn't want to risk losing focus now that she'd found her footing. A slight breeze from the bay cooled her sweaty face. Even so, she looked forward to a shower.

Olivia descended into the sun sparkling off the incredible Adriatic before her. She'd slipped on sunglasses but refused to glance sideways at the view along the length of the slope. Instead, she heard her karate instructor's voice in her head for the first time in years, exhorting her not to be distracted by the scenery but to stay focused on the task she'd set herself.

When she finally stepped onto Tabaćina Street, Olivia's sense of accomplishment took her by surprise. She hadn't realized how much she'd missed having a mission to complete, even if it was only a personal physical challenge. Then again, she'd always excelled athletically. Failing to conquer the trail immediately in the new shoes had apparently bruised her ego.

Though her thighs and , and her calves felt tight, Olivia pushed herself to run the short distance back to St. Tryphon Square. When she arrived, the sun warmed the ancient red stone of her apartment building, which sat on one side of the square across from the Baroque cathedral. At this hour, only a handful of locals, mostly employees of the restaurants setting up for breakfast and a few parishioners, populated the square.

Olivia took the short staircase to her studio apartment in three bounds, relishing the protest from her exhausted muscles.

As she opened the door to the apartment, her fluffy marmalade cat, Cleo, met her with a chiding *meow* and wrapped himself around her ankles in a vain attempt to bring her down to his level, the floor. Olivia, exhilarated from her success, scooped the cat up and laid him on her shoulder where his purrs of reconciliation told her that he'd forgiven her for being gone.

"Silly floof," said Olivia, rubbing a hand along his spine and nuzzling his side against her cheek.

Cleo, more hair than body, shoved his head against her face as he wiggled, trying to get closer to her neck.

Laughing, Olivia held him against her as she turned toward the poster bed along the outside wall of the studio apartment. Empty.

She heard the shower.

Walking the handful of meters to the bed, she disengaged the loudly purring cat and set him on the crumpled sheets. "Be right back."

Cleo meowed his disapproval as he sank against the down pillows.

"Oh, you'll live," said Olivia as she tugged off the foot gloves and then slipped her workout tank and shorts off, dropping them on the floor on her walk toward the bathroom.

She left the door open. The tiny white-tiled bathroom barely had room for a shower, toilet, and pedestal sink. But she could certainly squeeze into the curtained alcove with Étienne.

Without a word, she slipped inside the curtain.

Étienne, shampoo running down his face, pulled her against his chest. "It appears that I timed my shower well," he said, grinning.

"Indeed," she said, her gaze homing in on his mouth before she kissed him.

They made love, Étienne's long graceful fingers sure as he stroked over Olivia's wet skin. Afterwards, he washed her hair before working conditioner through it. Then he squeezed liquid soap into his palm and lathered her body, his gaze never leaving hers as his hands massaged their way down her tired back and tight buttocks. He held her head in a gentle grip as he rinsed her hair, letting the water sluice away the soap on her skin.

By the time they'd finished their shower, the water had grown tepid, and the bathroom had puddles.

Half an hour later, they walked hand-in-hand to their favorite restaurant in the square with a dozen tables under a large canopy. It wasn't yet open for tourists, but the owner, aware that Étienne often worked the early shift at the hospital, insisted that they eat breakfast there beforehand.

As they sat with their coffee waiting for eggs benedict and an omelet, Étienne said, "I heard from the Necker. They would like me to start in a few weeks."

Olivia's heart skipped a beat. She'd known that the Necker Hospital for Sick Children in Paris would jump at the chance to add a top-notch pediatric oncologist to their staff, but that had been a hazy future prospect. She swallowed.

Then she leaned forward and took Étienne's hand before kissing it. "That's fantastic!"

He tilted his head. His dark eyes gleamed. "I can delay my start date until you learn whether your transfer request is approved."

She shrugged. "You know how these things are, *mon amour*. I have yet to speak with the regional director. Her assistant says that she is traveling to all of the local clinics to review their procedures."

Étienne brought her hand to his mouth and kissed it in return. "You do not need a job waiting for you in Paris, *ma chérie*. Quit and come with me. I will support you until you find a suitable position. If nothing else, I am sure there is something available at the Necker."

Olivia blinked, nonplussed. "What are you saying? That I should leave HANDS Across Borders?"

"I am saying that I love you and do not want to live without you," said Étienne, still holding her hand as he slipped from his chair onto his knees next to the table. "Please say you will come, Olivia. You can care for women and children in France. There are many refugees from North Africa and the Middle East who need you."

Before Olivia could respond, he lifted something between his thumb and forefinger. A ring. "To sweeten my offer. Will you marry me, Olivia Markham?"

A loud ringing filled Olivia's ears. For a moment, she thought it came from her furiously beating heart, but then she realized that it was the cathedral bells tolling the top of the hour.

Her gaze dipped from Étienne's to the ring. The solitaire diamond snagged the early sunlight that filtered under the canopy, sparkling improbably.

Like her cherished dreams.

Olivia brought her gaze back to Étienne's and then took in his entire beloved visage. His dark hair, worn a little long, waved over his forehead and caressed the collar of his crisp button-down shirt. The slight crease between his eyebrows telegraphed anxiety. He really didn't know how she felt about him, did he?

Olivia leaned forward and smoothed a thumb over Étienne's forehead before tucking a lock of hair behind his ear. "Yes. Yes, I'll marry you."

A wide smile transformed Étienne's face, dislodging the lock of hair and making him look boyish. "*Je suis trop contente!*" he said as he grabbed Olivia's face and kissed her.

Behind him, the restaurant owner and staff clapped.

Étienne then slipped the ring onto Olivia's third finger on her left hand before kissing its palm and rising to return to his seat.

And, then, despite the magic of the moment, they ate their breakfast, Olivia digging into her omelet, and her new fiancé more calmly and carefully cutting up his eggs benedict.

Although the hospital provided parking for its staff, it was only a five-minute walk south in Škaljari. Olivia accompanied Étienne, holding his hand and kissing him goodbye before heading farther south on Route 2 towards the free clinic offering immunizations and health screenings that HANDS Across Borders operated.

It was also a CIA safehouse. And she was the housekeeper.

As Olivia approached the front door to the low concrete building that the Agency had purchased, a woman stepped out from the shadowy niche. It was Lejla, a Bosniak refugee who'd married a Moroccan in Turkey. She and her husband Ayman had come to Montenegro on their way to Germany where he had family. As with others in the increasing numbers of refugees from African and Asian countries, Lejla and her husband had planned to stay only a few days in the small coastal country until they could manage transportation elsewhere.

"Lejla!" said Olivia, stopping in front of the door. Smiling, she inclined her head. "*As-Salam-u-Alaikum.*"

Lejla tilted her head but didn't return Olivia's smile. "*Wa alaikum salaam.*"

"What's wrong?" asked Olivia in English, her own smile dissipating. "Is it Nika?"

After Olivia had suspected something amiss with Lejla and Ayman's two-year-old daughter Nika during a visit to get the family immunizations necessary to travel, she'd escorted them to the local hospital as their translator. It was how she'd met Étienne, who'd diagnosed the little girl with acute lymphoblastic leukemia. As a result, the family had settled in Kotor for the long-term, hosting other refugees.

"No, no," said Lejla, shaking her head. She darted a glance around her. "Please, can you come with me?" she asked. "There is someone who needs your help."

Olivia's gut stirred. She'd been in Kotor long enough that the refugee community, such as it was, knew about the free clinic. Locals brought newcomers for shots, free vitamins, and the occasional mammogram and ultrasound. Given Lejla's nervousness, there must be something more to the situation.

"Let me grab my bag first," she said, sensing that her small medical kit would likely be inadequate.

Lejla nodded and then remained outside the open doorway while Olivia packed first-aid items such as antiseptic, bandages, and topical antibiotics, into a duffel bag. She added a blood-pressure cuff, penlight, and stethoscope, throwing up a prayer that these basic items would suffice.

Even before Olivia had finished locking the clinic's front door, Lejla took off at a brisk pace, throwing glances around her the entire time that they walked toward her apartment building a kilometer southwest of HANDS Across Borders.

Once inside her apartment, she deadbolted the entry door behind them and led Olivia to one of the two bedrooms. When she opened the door, Olivia recognized Nika's bedroom, decorated with a riot of bright pink balloons and images of a pink-blob character named Barbapapa from an older French children's cartoon series. The little girl herself, however, wasn't present. Instead, a female form lay wrapped in an ankle-length *niqāb* on top of Nika's comforter, only her eyes visible. She didn't look at them but stared with unfocused eyes at the ceiling.

Lejla waited in the doorway. "This is my friend Merjem. She–she needs an exam only a woman doctor can give. But she cannot go to the hospital."

"What happened to her?" asked Olivia, stepping to the woman's side and taking her wrist. Her pulse, rapid and strong, leapt through the skin at Olivia's light palpation. Whatever had happened, its cruel memory still gripped her.

When Lejla didn't respond, Olivia looked at her. "You don't need to tell me more. I can guess. Was it her husband?"

Lejla shook her head. She visibly swallowed. When she answered, it was with her gaze trained on the floor between them. "A respected teacher visited their home last night," she whispered. "Merjem's husband offered her to him."

Alarm shot through Olivia at Lejla's words. Even so, she continued with a visual and external inspection. Angry bruises darkened the victim's wrists and, despite the concealing *niqāb* face covering, it was clear that one eye was swollen. Her pulse continued to bound, and her dilated pupils didn't respond to the penlight. Olivia didn't need to use the stethoscope to know that Merjem's heart raced, and her breathing was shallow.

Olivia tamped down her outrage. "Merjem," she said in a gentle voice. "May I look at your injuries? The ones that are hidden?"

Merjam said nothing.

Olivia sighed. "I can't force her, Lejla. It will only make matters worse. I can, however, give her a sedative. I'll need to return to the clinic for it."

Sedatives weren't a routine part of Olivia's cover with the NGO, but the safehouse had a fully stocked medicine cabinet. She had no trouble raiding it.

Lejla raised a troubled gaze, but this time she held Olivia's. "Merjam is pregnant. She has not yet told her husband. Will she lose the baby?"

Fury sparked inside Olivia, but she remained outwardly calm. "I don't know. But she needs the care of a doctor."

"No." Now Lejla's eyes flashed. What she said next shocked Olivia. "No doctor will treat her better than you do, *gospoda*, not even Dr. Dumond. The teacher is still at Merjam's house. Give her sanctuary. I know there are those who help women to leave their husbands when they are being hurt. I think you are one of them."

Olivia grasped the small disc hanging on a chain around her neck. It had warmed enough to burn against her palm.

She straightened her shoulders. "I am." She paused, dropping her hand. "But I can't help Merjam because you ask me. I need to hear her say that she wants to leave her husband. If she does, I'll do everything in my power to help her."

Before Lejla could respond, a heavy knocking came on the apartment door. Lejla's eyes widened.

"It is Merjam's husband," she said in a low, panicked voice. "He will make her go with him."

Olivia looked back at Merjam, whose gaze hadn't left the ceiling but whose hands now gripped her *niqāb* so tightly that her knuckles had whitened.

It was enough for Olivia. It had to be.

"Tell him that the nurse from the free clinic has come to meet with her privately so that she may maintain her modesty. Say that she suspects that she is with child and wishes to ensure her health for his sake."

Lejla's gaze searched Olivia's before she nodded. It was the only possible thing that she could say that would prevent Merjam's husband from barging into the apartment and dragging her away.

Olivia returned to Merjam's side and pulled out the blood-pressure cuff and stethoscope as Lejla scurried across the main room. Pushing the cloth of the *niqāb* up the supine woman's arm to expose it, she slipped the cuff on and appeared to listen to Merjam's blood pressure as Lejla opened the door. She didn't glance up until she heard voices.

Olivia raised her gaze to the men, who stood just outside the doorway to the apartment. Merjam's husband, a young man with a heavy dark beard and traditional Moroccan clothing, scowled at Lejla as he asked about his wife. But it was the middle-aged man with white hair and beard and a heavily lined face that suggested sorrow standing next to him that made Olivia's breath catch.

Mr. X.

The handler of the Islamic terrorists who'd bombed the Berlin Christmas market a year and a half ago. The terrorists who'd blown themselves up in Brussels, killing her friend Monica.

The handler who'd nearly trapped her when she'd foolishly gone after him on her own.

He turned to the man next to him, who listened to Lejla as she explained, head bowed, what Olivia had told her to say. As Mr. X moved, his embroidered white *taqiyah* caught Olivia's attention. Even from this distance, she recognized its pattern.

It was the same as the skullcap she'd found next to the dead woman in the Venetian palazzo on her last CIA operation.

The one where a Predator drone had been purchased by unknown interests.

TWO

Olivia's stomach muscles tightened. She was trapped inside a little girl's bedroom with a nearly catatonic rape victim and another woman, a civilian, within easy reach of the two males, who blocked access to the only exit. They didn't have to be trained to take her or hurt her. Kill her. Clearly Mr. X had the skills for that.

And Olivia had nothing with her besides her wits. No gun. No weapon at all. A housekeeper didn't carry a weapon into the field.

That didn't stop her frantic gaze cataloguing the items closest at hand. Unless she could blind them with the penlight or choke one with the stethoscope, she was SOL. Not even the tweezers or scissors would do much in this situation.

Her St. Michael medal burned against the fabric of her thin shirt.

Focus, Olivia came the voice of Sam Ahren, her first CIA handler, in her thoughts. *You can't help others unless you help yourself first. Never surrender yourself unless it's your only move. It's an OODA loop, remember? Sometimes the only decision you have is to keep observing.*

But Olivia wasn't so good at observing and orienting. She was much better at deciding and acting.

As soon as Sam's voice faded, Mr. X spoke. "*Subhanallah*, this is excellent news! You will be a father, Zouhair, *inshallah*. It is as I told you. Allah, *Al-Mumeet*, blesses our intentions and shows us the way forward. We will wait here until her exam is complete."

Oh, Sweet Lord.

Mr. X's gaze moved toward Merjam and Olivia, who dropped hers before it connected with his. She felt it linger on her as she pulled the Velcro strap on the blood-pressure cuff open and stowed her gear in the duffel bag that she'd brought. Chill flowed down her spine. What were the chances that his malevolent stare simply applied to a woman without a headscarf and not because he recognized her from the Berlin *shawarma* restaurant where they'd come face to face?

It was a tossup as far as Olivia was concerned. Mr. X probably looked at most Western women the same way. But it stood to reason that a meticulous sociopath like this terrorist leader would remember the defiant blonde who'd associated him with the rapes in the Wilhem Memorial Church just before the bomb went off on the plaza. What would he make of her appearance here? He had to know that she wasn't in German law enforcement....

As Lejla moved around her tiny kitchen preparing tea, Olivia bent over Merjam. "Please go to the hospital," she said in a low voice. "Ask for Dr. Étienne Dumond. Lejla knows him. He will get you the exams and tests that you need without telling your husband."

Olivia glanced into the apartment before taking the other woman's hand and squeezing it. "And then I will help you find a new home so that you and your baby will be safe."

The traumatized woman didn't respond.

Olivia waited a moment before picking up the duffel bag and squaring her shoulders. As she walked into the main room, Lejla carried a tray with tea toward the sitting area.

Olivia stopped halfway to the door. The men watched her through narrowed eyes.

"I will return later with the vitamins that I promised you," she said, hoping that Lejla would understand why she'd chosen not to mention the sedative. She swiveled toward the men and inclined her head. "*Ma'a salama.*"

Neither man acknowledged Olivia's goodbye, but neither did they attempt to stop her as she repeated her farewell to Lejla. No recognition sharpened Mr. X's gaze, and yet the hairs still stood on the back of Olivia's neck as she left. It went against all of her instinct and her training to turn her back on him.

He *had* referred to "The Inflictor of Death," one of Allah's ninety-nine names, when speaking to Merjam's husband.

Olivia returned to the clinic, dumping the duffel bag to the floor behind the front desk before entering her security passcode for the door into the back area. She wanted to get her gun and plenty of clips as well as the sedatives.

The secure phone started ringing while she rummaged through the stock of medicines.

Olivia halted, a little taken aback. In the year she'd been in Kotor, the secure phone had only rung two other times. The safehouse here wasn't a high-traffic facility for the CIA.

The phone stopped ringing and then started again. Olivia snapped out of her unaccountable reverie. Gripping a pharmaceutical package in one hand, she strode to the cabinet with the secure phone and picked it up mid-ring.

"Housekeeping," she said.

"We have a last-minute reservation."

Olivia's heartrate sped up. "ETA for check-in?"

"Sometime in the next twelve hours. Talbot Exports."

"Confirmed." Olivia hung up the phone, running a hand through her hair.

Protocol dictated that she stay at the site until after the 'guest' or 'guests' left. What were the chances that whoever it was would arrive before she got back from Lejla's apartment? If the reservation had an arrival window within the next hour, Langley would have specified that. She had time to deliver the sedatives to Lejla and find out where Merjam and her husband were staying in Kotor.

And do a little intelligence gathering.

Even if Mr. X moved locations frequently as she suspected, she could glean a few details about his movements, resources, and communications to add to the file she'd started in Berlin.

Stuffing the meds into a small bag, Olivia went to the weapons safe and removed a Glock 19 along with extra clips. After checking the clip already in the weapon, she put another two into the bag. It wasn't ideal, but she didn't really have another way to carry extra ammunition. It was June, and she was dressed in a flowery skirt.

She could tuck a knife into the back of her waistband, though

....

Olivia opened the left drawer on the desk in the operations room and pulled out a small Indonesian fighting knife called a *karambit*. Given that the blade on the little knife was about two-and-a-half inches, it wouldn't do much damage in untrained hands. But Olivia had trained with it. She knew exactly how to use a karambit with lethal force.

She hurried back to Lejla's apartment, refraining from running now that it was mid-morning, and more people ventured out into Kotor's streets. Tourism, especially from cruise ships, provided the economic backbone of this small Adriatic port city, and locals now made their way to Old Town to greet the first of the day's visitors. Olivia didn't want to draw attention.

But when she arrived, no one answered the door.

A sense of foreboding flooded Olivia, but there was nothing that she could do except return to the clinic and await the CIA reservation.

A shadow fell across her path as she left the apartment building.

It was Mr. X. The look of pure malice on his face told her that he knew exactly who she was and why she'd returned. He stood watching her, his hands clasped behind his back.

Olivia halted. "Where is she?"

She didn't bother to deliver the customary Arabic greeting wishing peace upon him. Instead, she scanned the area around them for threats. As far as she could tell, they were alone. No sense of watching eyes disturbed the hair on the back of her neck.

He ignored her question. "You do not have your friends here in Kotor, do you?" His eyes narrowed as they raked her from head to toe. "It is no surprise that Allah wills our meeting."

"Perhaps," said Olivia, the warm medal on her chest vibrating as she spoke. "Are you so certain of the outcome?" She wished that she held the Glock.

He inhaled sharply, his nostrils flaring as if he smelled something rank. "Everything that comes from the mouth of an unbeliever is an abomination to Allah." He took a step toward her, his fist clenched.

Olivia tensed.

Mr. X came close enough that a pungent blend of tobacco, sweat, and cooking spices assailed her nose. Then a babble of voices in the distance pierced the miasma.

Mr. X glanced at the street around them as if remembering where they were. He looked back at Olivia. "We will meet again, demon."

"Count on it," said Olivia, holding his gaze. "Better bring *your* friends because I fight back."

Mr. X moved past, his striped cotton *djellaba*, the traditional Moroccan outer hooded robe, floating behind his swift steps. Something about his tanned forearms brought up images of him beating Merjam. Olivia had to swallow the bile that rose to her throat.

She returned to the clinic feeling on edge, her nerves strung tight.

Her earlier elation about Étienne's proposal had evaporated in the harsh light of reality. Now all she could think about was Merjam and Lejla. Was Lejla's absence ominous or coincidental? Had Merjam seen a doctor? If she'd gone to Étienne as Olivia had urged, he would have called Olivia.

At four that afternoon, Olivia called Étienne. Faking nonchalance, she said, "Hey, listen, I've got some bad news."

"What is that?" he asked, a slight tone of alarm sharpening his voice. "You've changed your mind about marrying me, *ma chérie*?"

Olivia refrained from sighing. "*Mais non*. It's just that I have to stay late tonight. The regional director has come on a surprise visit and wants to go through my records with a magnifying glass. I fear that she plans to shut down the clinic."

"Ah, *non*! That would be terrible." He paused. "But it would make your departure less painful, *n'est-ce pas*?"

Olivia gripped her cellphone and looked out the front window of the clinic where a young Montenegrin family walked, a little girl holding her father's hand while her mother pushed an umbrella stroller with a sleeping toddler.

Perhaps that would be her and Étienne someday....

"That's true," she said to his question about leaving the clinic, "but I can't think of my own happiness when I'm worried about Nika. How is she doing?"

"Remarkably. She was here this morning with her father. I have cleared her for travel and arranged treatment for her in Berlin. Put that worry out of your mind."

Olivia sighed. That was good news. "I'll try not to be too late."

"I will keep dinner warm for you."

"I'd rather you kept the bed warm."

"For you, anything," said Étienne. He sounded like he meant it.

Olivia knew what the answer was to her next question, but still she asked it. "Have you seen any *unusual* cases today? You know, a referral?"

"No one," said Étienne. Olivia heard the frown in his voice. "What are you not telling me?"

"Nothing. Never mind. I'll see you later."

Étienne sighed but said nothing.

"Étienne?"

"*Oui?*"

"I love you."

"I love you, too, Olivia."

Olivia had to find something productive to do with her time while she waited for Talbot Exports to arrive. If she couldn't immediately help Merjam, reviewing what she knew about Mr. X made sense.

For the next few hours, Olivia read through the file on the Berlin and Brussels bombings that she'd surreptitiously copied and carried with her after being reassigned, first to Prague and now to Kotor. It was the first time that she'd studied it after meeting Étienne and resigning herself to a peripheral field assignment. She didn't know if she liked being dragged back into the world of terrorism now that a normal life beckoned.

Olivia had annotated the contraband file with her unsanctioned investigation into the concurrent gang rape at the Kaiser Wilhelm Memorial Church. She'd tied the victim to a restaurant that one of the bombers frequented. From there, Olivia looked for a direct connection. Although her team leader for the Berlin mission had suspected a shadowy *jihadi* handler, it was Olivia who'd transformed that gut feeling into a flesh-and-blood man. But not a name.

Olivia pulled out the photos of Mr. X that a mysterious source had left in her Prague apartment. She'd never bothered to share the folder of intelligence in which they'd been included with Reardon, the Prague station chief. Not only would it open up a can of worms regarding the Italians, it would likely send Reardon on an internal hunt, compromising her source. What it would *not* do was find the Predator drone stolen from the Italian air force or identify the mastermind behind the Berlin and Brussels attacks.

At 9:30 p.m., the concealed buzzer at the clinic door sounded in the secure operations room. Olivia looked at the screen for the security camera on the main door. A hard-looking man stared into it. She recognized him. Miles Baxter. One of the CIA's most effective recovery experts. His team had gone after the *hawaladar* broker in Berlin who'd helped finance the *jihadis*.

She went through the safehouse protocol anyway and depressed the intercom button. "Reservations."

"Do you have a room?"

"Account?"

"Miles Baxter, Talbot Exports. B-A-X-T-E-R."

Olivia repeated the information back to the operative. "Baxter, Talbot Exports. B-A-X-T-E-R. Your reservation has been confirmed, Mr. Baxter."

She remotely unlocked the clinic door and jumped up to stuff the unauthorized dossier out of sight into her personal duffel bag before racing to open the inner door to the secure area.

A moment later Baxter dragged a hooded man, bound hand and foot with security cuffs connected by a chain, into the safehouse. Another hard-looking man holding a combat shotgun followed them. They weren't looking for a comfortable place for an asset to rest and recuperate in safety.

They needed to wring intelligence from a bad actor.

"I'm Markham," she said.

Baxter acknowledged this with a scant nod. "Where's our room?" he asked.

"Down the hall to the right," said Olivia, stepping back next to the wall so that Baxter could pass with his prisoner.

The man with the weapon followed without a glance her way.

Two more armed men had entered the front of the clinic behind the first three. One took up station in the clinic's waiting room with a large duffel bag next to him. Olivia knew a third man waited outside watching the perimeter.

Their prisoner must be high value. And high risk.

Olivia went back into the operations room where a two-way mirror showed the interrogation room. Baxter had chained the prisoner's hands to a metal ring on the table and removed his hood. Olivia, eyes narrowed, leaned closer to the mirror. The cold stare of the bearded man sitting at the table sent a shiver of presentiment down her spine. His clothing and demeanor reminded her of Zouhair, Merjam's husband. All at once she knew why Mr. X had appeared in Kotor.

He was interested in this man.

The operator wielding the combat shotgun appeared in the doorway. "Linen closet?"

Olivia's heart thumped. "Right across the hall behind you." She lifted her chin in his direction as she answered.

"Kill the cameras in that room," he said as he pivoted.

With cold fingers, Olivia did as he ordered. Now whatever Baxter planned to do to the prisoner wouldn't be recorded.

Two minutes later, Baxter's men appeared in the interrogation room with a towel and a bucket of water. They unchained the prisoner from the table.

The restrained man sneered at Baxter. "I don't fear you, American," he said in accented English.

Olivia listened intently. What was it? Turkish? Bosniak?

Baxter leaned closer to the prisoner, his stare drilling the other man. "You seem to think you'll withstand whatever I do to you. But you won't. You won't last five minutes. And then you'll tell me everything you know about the others in your group, your resources, your communications methods, who gives the orders."

The prisoner said nothing.

"Bring him down," said Baxter.

One of Baxter's men tilted the chair back on two legs while the other poured water from the bucket over the prisoner's towel-draped face. He shuddered and thrashed as water cascaded, soaking the towel that clung to his mouth and nose.

Olivia's heart hammered in her chest.

"Bring him up," said Baxter. "Had enough, Esad?"

Esad, spluttering, spit a mouthful of water at Baxter.

"Okay then. Take him down," said Baxter, gesturing at his men.

The whole cycle began again with one man tipping the chair back as the other doused the choking prisoner.

After an eternity of ten seconds, the chair dropped to all four feet. This time when Baxter tugged the soaking towel from Esad's head, his pale, wet face told its own story.

"I can take whatever you give," he said, his weak delivery at odds with his words.

Baxter had other ideas. He looked at one of the men. "Get me a knife."

Something in Olivia's peripheral vision caught her attention. She glanced down. All of the security camera screens had gone blank. *Oh shit.*

Mr. X had figured out who she was and followed her.

Grabbing her gun from the weapons cabinet, she jumped up and ran into the hall. But before she could get to the door to the interrogation room, the operative in the clinic appeared in the doorway to the secure area.

"Baxter!" he shouted. "We've got company!"

Baxter gestured toward the man holding the chair back. "Greggs, stay with him." He looked at the other man with the bucket. "Lowe, let's go."

The two recovery experts brushed past Olivia without a glance. She looked into the interrogation room where Greggs stood over the panting Esad. Her gaze connected with the bound man. He clearly knew who assaulted the safehouse.

On impulse, Olivia stepped into the room. Ignoring Greggs, she addressed Esad in Maghrebi Arabic. "I saw Zouhair and his wife Merjam this morning."

He blinked. Then he lunged from his chair, yelling, "You lie! Merjam would never marry Zouhair."

Esad's reaction signaled a concern for Merjam that came from a close relationship. Whether he was Merjam's brother or sweetheart didn't matter.

Greggs grasped Esad and wrenched him back into the chair. He punched the prisoner, and while the other man's head lolled on his neck, he reattached the cuffs to the ring on the table.

The other CIA officer glared at Olivia. "Who the hell are Zouhair and Merjam? How do you know the package?"

Shouting and the sound of glass breaking filtered in from the front room. Automatic gunfire rocked the night beyond the clinic. The security door must have been left open.

Gregg's gaze shot to the doorway to the hall.

Olivia kept her focus on Esad. She shook her head. "I do not lie. This is a real clinic. I was called to treat Merjam, who had been raped and beaten." She left out who had done these things. "She is also pregnant, but I had to leave her. I do not know if she has been to the hospital to make sure that she and the baby are well."

Now Esad howled and tugged so hard on the chain holding him to the table that it shook.

From the front of the clinic, Baxter shouted, "Greggs, get out here! Bring the other bag!"

Greggs hammered Olivia with a pointed glare. "You. You're the housekeeper. He's your guest. You know what that means."

Olivia nodded. Esad was now her responsibility.

Greggs tossed Olivia a set of keys before snatching up a large, heavy bag and disappearing. He'd scarcely been gone thirty seconds when someone yelled "grenade!"

And then an explosion rocked the clinic.

THREE

The two-way mirror on the wall cracked. Concrete dust rained from the ceiling, and smoke choked the hallway from the clinic. A hoarse scream tore the heavy air followed by more gunfire.

They had to get out of this room.

Dashing to Esad, Olivia unlocked the chain from the ring on the table. She stepped back and pointed the gun muzzle at him. "Let's go."

He narrowed his eyes. "Why? They want me. You they will kill."

Olivia cocked her head. "That may be, but I'll kill you first."

Esad dragged his gaze from the top of her head to her feet. Olivia knew that all he saw was the white cotton blouse and the floral skirt. He said nothing.

Olivia shot him. It was a careful shot to his shoulder where the damage would be minimal, provided she got him swift medical attention. But she couldn't drag a bigger, heavier man with her who didn't believe that she'd use her weapon.

"Get up," she said, holding the gun in an unwavering, two-handed grip. "Every wound becomes life threatening if you don't stop the bleeding."

Groaning, Esad pressed a palm against the bleeding hole in his shoulder. "I will only go with you if you take me to Merjam," he said through clenched teeth.

Rough male voices speaking Arabic sounded from the clinic. Olivia had no time to think about Esad's demand or whether she could actually comply.

She nodded. Esad struggled to his feet.

"Wait a moment until I can check the hallway," said Olivia, peering around the doorframe.

Someone had closed the security door. That was something at least. It would take a grenade or shaped charge to get through the reinforced steel and concrete walls.

She glanced back at her white-faced 'guest.' "Follow me."

Esad lowered his head and shuffled forward. Olivia didn't wait to make sure that he stayed with her. Instead, she turned right outside the interrogation room and headed to the rear exit. If they were really lucky, the attackers hadn't made it into the narrow alley behind the building or she was in for a very short walk. But some forward-thinking CIA resource manager had made sure that the entrances to the alley had been hidden behind decorative screens, and no one waited to surprise them.

It was dark in the unlit alley. Olivia headed west toward the neighboring street where she could steal a car. Even outside the back of the clinic, explosives and gunpowder scented the humid June evening, although the gunfire had stopped. Somewhere in the distance came the sound of sirens. Someone had called the police.

Telling Esad to wait behind the decorative screen, Olivia sprinted across the street to a line of parked cars. The first two that she tried were locked. The third, an older gray Citroen, wasn't.

She motioned for Esad, who lumbered across the street to the front passenger door, falling heavily into the seat while Olivia took the time to search for a spare key. They really didn't have time for her to locate jumper cables to bypass the ignition switch or to dismantle the steering column to hotwire the car. Nothing was as fast or as easy as it looked in the movies.

Her guardian angel was looking out for her. The car's owner had left a key in the empty ashtray. Sixty seconds later they were traveling toward Lejla's apartment.

When they arrived, Olivia turned to Esad. "Stay here. The woman who lives here knows how to find Merjam."

She didn't wait for Esad's response. He was slumped against the side window anyway.

Ayman answered Olivia's knock.

"Olivia *Hanım*!" he said, surprise making his voice rise. "What are you doing here? It is late." He shifted back and forth, glancing over his shoulder. The perfunctory greeting wishing her peace remained unspoken.

Olivia had spent many hours in Ayman's presence over the previous year as he waited with Nika at the hospital or in this very apartment while he and Lejla hosted her for tea. She recognized nervousness.

"Please forgive me, Ayman *Bey*," she said. "But I must speak with Lejla about Merjam."

"Lejla is caring for Nika," he said, his gaze anywhere but on Olivia's face. "She got sick after this morning's treatment."

She heard murmuring from inside the apartment.

"I'm sorry to hear that, but I would not ask if it was not extremely important. I need to find Merjam, not only to make sure that she is safe and well, but because I have a message for her from Esad."

As Olivia had suspected, that name elicited a response.

"Esad!" The shout came from the sitting area followed by rapid whispering.

A moment later, Lejla pulled the door wide. Olivia could see Merjam sitting on the sofa under the window. Wide dark eyes stared at Olivia as her hands clutched at the cloth of her *niqāb* bunched at her waist. A large fabric bag sat on the floor by her feet.

"Please, come in, Olivia," said Lejla, peering outside the apartment door both ways.

Despite her gut screaming at her to keep moving, to get Esad medical attention, to contact Langley for instructions, Olivia stepped inside. Ayman shut the door behind her.

Olivia ignored Lejla and Ayman to focus on Merjam. "I don't have a lot of time, so forgive my bluntness. Esad has been shot, and he waits outside in a car."

Crying out, Merjam stood.

Lejla put a hand on Olivia's forearm. "Merjam agreed to let me take her to the hospital to be examined. But we had to wait until Zouhair and the teacher left for the evening. Please. This will be her only chance."

Olivia looked at first Lejla and then Ayman before returning to Lejla. "I suspect that you know more about Zouhair and the teacher than you've shared. You're not at all shocked that Esad's been shot."

She gestured toward Merjam. "That bag at Merjam's feet suggests that she plans to leave Kotor tonight."

Lejla shifted her feet but said nothing.

"Please trust me. I have resources that you do not. I can get her to safety out of Montenegro, but it will be better for you and Ayman if you cannot tell Zouhair or the teacher anything if you do not know the details."

"We must think of Nika," said Ayman to his wife.

Lejla's dark eyes studied Olivia. After a moment, she nodded.

Olivia looked to Merjam. "Please hurry, Merjam! Esad needs a doctor. Lejla, I need some clean towels."

Merjam nodded and picked up her bag. Two minutes later, Olivia raced toward Old Town and Étienne. Esad had lost consciousness, but Merjam found the fortitude to press a folded towel against his bleeding shoulder during the short drive to Olivia's apartment. Olivia parked on a side street and then took the stairs to the second floor at a run. She didn't have her cellphone or keys, so she was forced to knock on her own door.

Étienne opened it wearing a robe and boxers, a medical journal in one hand. "Olivia! What has happened?" he asked in alarm, gesturing at her blouse.

Olivia looked down. Esad's blood stained the white fabric. "It's not mine," she said, stepping into the apartment. "But he needs a doctor, and I can't take him to the emergency room."

Étienne studied her for a moment. Then he shook his head. "I am a pediatric oncologist. It has been some time since I practiced emergency medicine." He didn't ask why she couldn't take a bleeding man to the ER.

"Then help me get supplies. I can stop the bleeding and give him a transfusion."

Olivia watched Étienne as he blinked, absorbing what she'd just told him. He knew that she'd been trained as an EMT as an undergrad, but EMTs typically didn't insert IVs.

Her fiancé nodded. "I will get dressed."

As he pulled on pants and a T-shirt, Olivia knelt next to the bed and pulled out a storage bin. Inside she had a backup weapon, spare clips, cash, burner phone, and duplicate IDs. It wasn't exactly a go-bag, but her previous training had ingrained the need for emergency preparedness. She tossed the items into a backpack and stood, only to find Étienne watching her open mouthed.

"I'll explain later," she said before he could ask any questions.

They hustled outside to the stolen Citroen where Merjam still knelt in the backseat pressing the soaked towel into Esad's shoulder. As Olivia explained to the other woman that Étienne was a doctor, he took over, compressing a fresh towel against the wound. Then Olivia got behind the wheel.

"Brace yourselves," she said before accelerating through the narrow streets of Old Town.

Despite the desperate situation, the adrenaline coursing through Olivia's veins made her feel alive in a way that she hadn't felt in a year. Her vision and hearing had a keen edge, lending a supernatural vividness to the night. She slowed her breathing, channeling her nervous energy into deliberate action.

Welcome to the greatest show on earth. Olivia almost laughed as Sam Ahren's voice played in her thoughts.

Though it wasn't late, there wasn't much traffic in the small port city. They arrived at the hospital in record time. Olivia parked twenty meters down the street from the main entrance.

They managed to get Esad to come around enough to get out of the car. He leaned on Étienne and Olivia as he stumbled toward the building. Merjam followed. They stopped at the side of the hospital where Esad could prop himself against the outside wall, panting and shiny-faced in the warm streetlight.

Étienne looked at Olivia. "No one goes into the main hospital at this hour. You two can get him inside while I distract security. Take him to an exam room in oncology. I will meet you there."

Before Étienne could act, however, a vehicle careened to a stop across from the main entrance. The driver got out and ran toward the door. It was Baxter.

Thirty seconds later, two orderlies trotted out with a gurney and began to extract another man from the passenger seat.

Olivia swallowed, hard. What had happened to the rest of the team? Surely the two men outside on the perimeter and overwatch had survived the attack. But the wounded man's injuries must be life threatening for Baxter to risk coming to the local hospital.

What had happened to the attackers?

Esad groaned, bringing her attention back to her situation.

She gestured toward the group at the car. The hospital's lone security guard had come out and now watched as the orderlies lifted a badly wounded man onto the gurney.

"Someone's looking out for us. Let's go now while the guard has his attention elsewhere."

Olivia and Étienne helped Esad while Merjam opened the front door. They'd barely reached the elevator that would take them to the oncology department before the security guard, orderlies, and newcomers came through the entrance. Olivia's gaze brushed Baxter's as she stepped inside the elevator car.

Ten minutes later, Étienne had removed Esad's shirt while Olivia started an IV. Merjam, silent and stiffly upright, watched from a corner of the exam room.

Her fiancé looked at Olivia as he cleaned the wound. "He's been shot. He should be admitted."

Olivia shook her head. "No one must know that he's here."

Étienne said nothing more while he worked to stabilize Esad, whose blood loss required a transfusion. The 9mm bullet had tumbled inside Esad's upper body on its way out his back—likely hitting his scapula and cracking it—but Olivia didn't have time for a full workup on the internal damage. She regretted shooting him. She hadn't fired a gun beyond the weekly practice at a range outside the capital Podgorica since the strange mission in Venice last year, the one that she'd undertaken while on disciplinary leave. Thank God she hadn't done any more damage to Esad than she had.

Olivia stepped into the hall while Étienne finished up with Esad. She needed to contact someone at Langley.

She powered the burner phone on. *Damn!* Its battery was only at twenty percent. She'd gotten lax about keeping it charged. At least she still knew the number to dial.

"Ops Center," said the cool voice on the other end of the line.

"Juliet Romeo Eight Juliet Zulu Two," said Olivia, supplying the required code phrase.

"Your phone isn't secure."

Olivia exhaled in exasperation. She refrained from snapping at the operator. "I don't have access to a secure phone."

"Go ahead." The operator sounded reluctant.

"This is Markham. 9-Alpha's been hit. Baxter's team has suffered heavy casualties."

"I need you to repeat that, please." Now the operator sounded incredulous. "Say again."

Olivia wanted to snarl. "The safe house has been breached. Baxter's team has taken casualties."

"Stand by." The line went silent. After what seemed like forever but was probably only a minute, the operator returned. "Transferring to Control."

Yes, transfer me for the love of all that's holy thought Olivia, pacing the hallway away from the exam room.

"George." Olivia didn't recognize the female voice on the other end of the line.

"This is Markham," she said again. "The safe house has been breached. Baxter's team is out of commission."

"What's your location?"

"I'm at the Kotor City Hospital. Baxter and one of his team are here, too."

"What about the location of the guest?"

"We escaped."

"Clarify. Do you have the guest?"

Olivia reached the end of the hall and pivoted. As she did, she saw Étienne standing at the other end, his arms crossed, watching her. She hadn't heard him come out of the exam room. That wasn't like her. She didn't usually let herself get so preoccupied.

"Yes! We got out. He's been shot. We're at the hospital now."

"Hold for further instructions."

Olivia studied the man she planned to marry, her thoughts racing. How much had Étienne heard? Enough, if his narrowed eyes and crossed arms indicated anything.

George came back on the line. "Stay there. We have an STU in transit. ETA is 2400 local time. They will take custody of the guest. You and Baxter will travel with them to Rome for a debrief."

"What about the clinic?" asked Olivia.

"A team is on the way to scrub it."

Olivia's heart lurched. *Damn.* That meant that Langley was closing the safe house location. She was being recalled.

"Copy that," she said, staring at Étienne.

"When were you going to tell me the truth?" he asked after Olivia ended the call. "After we were married? Do you really love me, Olivia? Is that even your name?"

Olivia swallowed around her suddenly thick throat.

"Yes," she said. It was almost a whisper. "My name is Olivia. And I really love you."

"Yet you were not going to tell me that the NGO is a sham. That you work instead for the Central Intelligence Agency. Am I right? What other organization has a 'safehouse' masquerading as a clinic run by a woman with a gun under her bed?"

"HANDS Across Borders isn't a sham. I really do help immigrants with immunizations and health screenings," said Olivia, hurt piercing her chest. This couldn't be happening. Not now.

"But you were not going to quit your real job as a spy to work at the Necker." There was disdain in his voice. And something else. Hurt.

Olivia shook her head. She didn't know what to say.

"Who are they?" he asked, tilting his head toward the exam room where Merjam and Esad waited.

"The less you know about them, the better." She took a deep breath. "In fact, it's probably best if you tell anyone who asks that we're no longer seeing each other." As she said this, she reflexively played with the engagement ring on her hand.

"Why?" Now Étienne looked angry. "What will the CIA do to me?"

Before Olivia could answer, Merjam came out of the exam room, her eyes wide in the opening of the *niqāb*. "He is here. Imam Alami has found us. I saw him when I looked outside the window."

A cold thrill shot through Olivia. Until now, she hadn't had a name for her nemesis, but the fact that he had the same last name as one of the Islamic suicide bombers on her last official mission couldn't be a coincidence. How had he tracked them to the hospital?

"We'll have to continue this later," she said to Étienne, who clearly understood the urgency of the situation because he straightened, the anger replaced by alertness.

They followed Merjam back into the exam room. Esad rested, pale and eyes closed, against the back of the exam chair. Étienne had helped him put his shirt back on and slipped his arm into a sling. Olivia went to the window where she peered out from the side.

Down below, in the narrow terrace in front of the hospital sat two older model cars. Several armed men stood outside the vehicles. One man stood alone: Imam Alami. He stared at the window to the exam room as he spoke to the armed men.

Crap. At this hour, none of the other hospital rooms had lights on.

"We've got to get to get out of here," said Olivia to Merjam and Esad. She looked at Étienne. "Can you show me another way out of the hospital that avoids the main entrance?"

He nodded.

Olivia, who'd tucked her weapon into the waist of her skirt, wished she'd worn something else. She also wished that she had a submachine gun and an ammo belt, but that was neither here nor there. Étienne slipped a shoulder under Esad's good arm, and with Merjam trailing behind the men, Olivia took up the rear position, the gun now gripped in one hand.

As they entered the hall, a massive orderly with the most vivid blue eyes that Olivia had ever seen pushed a cart piled with clean hospital gowns and other necessities toward them. It was odd, but when he offered to help Esad, Olivia accepted their good fortune. They avoided the elevators to take the stairs, and the orderly appeared to carry Esad the whole way.

At the first floor, Étienne left them to go to the pharmacy while Olivia and the other three exited the hospital through the rear entrance. The stolen car waited down a side street in view of the main entrance, so Olivia asked the orderly to bring it. Étienne arrived with a small bag at the same time as the car.

While the orderly helped Esad into the backseat next to Merjam, Étienne handed the bag to her.

"I grabbed some codeine and amoxicillin," he said. "But your friend really needs to have follow-up care with a doctor, Olivia."

She nodded. "Thank you." An awkward pause followed before she swallowed and said, "I'll call you when I can."

She leaned forward to kiss him goodbye, but as she did, Étienne reached both hands to hold the sides of her face. He searched her gaze and then scanned her face as if memorizing it. Before she could speak, he kissed her forehead and stepped an arms' length away.

"Be careful. If you have to shoot one of those terrorists following you, aim for the head or the heart this time."

Étienne spun on his heel and walked away from the car, blending into the shadows along the edge of the buildings across the narrow street as if he'd been trained to evade surveillance.

Watching him go, Olivia's bruised heart nearly stopped her breath. Absently, she rubbed at her sore chest.

"I really need to return to my duties," said the orderly in a pleasing baritone next to her, shifting to go back into the hospital.

Olivia started from her reverie and grabbed the giant's arm before he could take a step. He looked down at her with a raised brow.

Wow. His eyes gleamed so brightly that she imagined his gaze illuminated the shadows around them.

She shook her head to clear the wayward fancy. "Don't go back into the hospital. Armed men came into the building a few minutes ago. You won't be safe."

His eyes widened, but strangely Olivia didn't read fear there. An electric current seemed to snap into a nimbus around him. He nodded and turned to head down the narrow street away from them.

Satisfied, Olivia slid behind the wheel of the still-running Citroen and, engaging the clutch, popped the vehicle into gear. The car growled to life and shot forward. The image of the orderly in the rear-view mirror disappeared as Olivia took the next corner without slowing down.

She didn't see the giant halt when the car's taillights winked out as it sped away to safety.

Nor would she have believed her eyes an instant later when he'd entered the hospital, his entire form blazing white and his gaze filled with murder.

FOUR

With innate aplomb that covert training had only enhanced, Alžběta Czerná trailed her boss, a Polish organized-crime lord, and his girlfriend through Silesia Park in Chorzów. Beta had never had more than a few awkward dates, so she had no personal standard against which to measure the human mating dance, but it had always struck her as grossly offensive or at best highly implausible that such an attractive woman would let anyone as vile as Kacper Bryk take her on a romantic outing let alone lay hands on her. And yet, here they were, wandering hand-in-hand toward the outdated planetarium built in 1955 to honor Polish astronomer Nicholaus Copernicus.

Bryk and his girlfriend reached the top of the steep flight of concrete steps leading to the entrance of the planetarium, which was set on a low hill in the park. Beta halted on the side of the wide promenade leading to the steps, pretending to read the facility signage. From her peripheral vision, she saw Bryk scan the area around the dome as he ushered his girlfriend, hand on her lower back, inside.

Beta remained relaxed as his sharp gaze traveled toward her. She didn't actually fear that the canny crime boss would recognize her in the bright-yellow floral sundress, jean jacket, floppy straw hat, and sunglasses. She'd hidden her lustrous dark curls under an ash-blond wig and wore wedge sandals. Too, she'd changed her posture to that of bored college girl, slouching and chewing gum. To further mask her appearance, she chose to peer into the large straw tote bag hanging from her shoulder as he looked at her. All that Bryk saw was the crown of the hat.

A moment later, Bryk and his girlfriend disappeared.

Beta was about to jog up the staircase when a hard-looking man passed by her and took the wide concrete steps with large strides. She studied him as he did.

Although he wore a black sleeveless T-shirt and jeans, the prolific tattoos on his exposed arms and neck signaled that he had others. Given their increasing popularity, she couldn't be sure that the stranger had been inside a Russian prison, but she recognized the snake coiled around human remains on one arm. That meant a 'legitimate' thief in the criminal parlance. Not someone who pretended for social credit with other thugs.

Beta had also glimpsed a skull and crossbones, handgun, knife, and the letter 'K' on the back of his hand. So, a killer as well. Good to know.

What else had he done or achieved in the Russian underworld? Did he have eyes on his torso to show that he watched over others, the traditional role of the enforcer? Perhaps he even had eight-pointed stars emblazoned on his shoulders signaling that he held a position of authority over other thugs. What were the odds he'd arrived in time for the noon lightshow?

Beta waited until the stranger disappeared inside the planetarium before hurrying up the terraced steps. Once inside, she glanced around the dilapidated facility to ensure that Bryk and his girlfriend hadn't chosen to wander outside for a last-minute smoke or headed into the small observatory. As she expected, the entrance hall was empty save for the single employee waiting behind the service desk for stragglers. Beta bought a ticket and hurried into the theater.

The doors clicked shut behind her. Now no one would be able to enter for the next hour. As the lights dimmed, Beta, whose keen eyesight had no trouble adjusting, searched the auditorium. Although it could hold nearly 400 audience members, only a scattered handful filled the seats on this warm June afternoon. Bryk and his girlfriend sat directly opposite the Zeiss projector in the middle row under the 23-meter-dome—not exactly a popular position. The menacing stranger reclined alone in a seat behind and to the left of Bryk.

Nothing happened between Bryk and the other man during the show, which was dedicated to "Legends of the Night Sky" and recounted the mythological tales of constellations. Beta, who'd taken a seat in a row behind her target, ignored it to watch the trio from the periphery of her vision. Afterwards, the stranger stood and left the theater quickly. Beta dawdled long enough to see Bryk reach under the seat next to him. When he stood, he slipped his hand into his pocket.

The stranger and Bryk had just executed a brush pass as well as any seasoned operatives.

Bryk's gaze brushed Beta's as she turned to leave her seat. She felt its hot animosity between her shoulder blades. And then his girlfriend rescued her.

"That was amazing!" she said in Polish. "I'm so happy you brought me here today instead of some creepy warehouse in Katowice."

Beta, carrying her straw hat, sauntered from the theater ahead of them. She wandered toward the observatory, feeling Bryk's gaze on her the entire time. Now was the trickiest part of the operation. She couldn't slip away too quickly without feeding his innate paranoia, but she also couldn't allow him to observe her too closely.

The girlfriend saved her again. "Why do you keep looking at her? Do you know her?" Hostility sharpened her tone.

Beta resisted the urge to look over her shoulder. Instead, she stopped in front of a lighted display showing the solar system and pretended to read how the observatory's telescope worked.

Behind her, Bryk answered in a conciliatory tone. "I'm not looking at her, my love. I'm squinting in the light trying to see what's outside where I can smoke."

The girlfriend scoffed, but the couple passed by Beta and continued outside toward the large courtyard with its sundial. Beta dug into her tote bag until the door had closed behind them before slipping her sunglasses on and pivoting to walk out the entrance. Below her on the path toward the parking lot, she glimpsed the Russian enforcer.

She'd just discovered who Bryk had found to replace her in his sex-trafficking business.

Later that afternoon, Beta sat drinking Trebitsch in her booth, the half-empty bottle on the table next to a glass tumbler. She'd long since given up trying to drown her sorrows with the potent Czech alcohol, which Bryk mocked her for drinking. She'd never gotten drunk in her life. Somehow her body burned through even the strongest liquor before she felt much beyond a slight buzz. That fact had stood her in good stead when several dates had tried to ply her with alcohol in order to lower her defenses in their favor. Once, it had even meant the difference between rape and her kicking the shit out of the fool.

Unfortunately, it meant that she sat, stone-cold sober, pondering her failure to stop Bryk from resurrecting his business selling people into sexual slavery.

Grimacing, she tossed the Trebitsch back, savoring its burn down her throat. She deserved this. She'd been lulled into thinking that Bryk had abandoned that avenue of illicit revenue after she and the American woman had hijacked his shipment last summer. Bryk had been apoplectic for weeks, turning over everything inside his organization while searching for the competitor who'd dared to steal from him.

Although he'd found nothing, leaving her cover intact, he'd cut large numbers of low-level players from his roster and grown even more secretive. Beta, he'd kept as a manager of his bar, The Wild Stallion, and sent on occasional collections jobs when other employees had failed.

To make matters worse, she'd recently glimpsed a crate stamped with the identifiers of the Czech arms manufacturer Česká zbrojovka in the rear of Bryk's armored Mercedes Sprinter van. In the midst of this delicate operational dance, Beta had discovered that Bryk had returned to running girls. And now boys. Some as young as seven or eight.

Bile rose in Beta's throat, burning it in a way the Trebitsch couldn't. She poured another large draft into her glass and swallowed it, fighting fire with fire.

If she hadn't returned to the small pharmacy that Bryk had sent her to collect from so that she could leave a donation for the desperate owner, she might never have seen Bryk leaving the apartment above the small drugstore.

The apartment with several young women the Polish mafia boss kept for himself.

Beta shook her head. She wished she had her karambit, a small hooked Indonesian fighting knife. She'd often manipulated its blade mechanism one handed, alternating it between hands. The action soothed the beast in her. But she'd given it to the American. The one who'd sidetracked her from her true mission for Czech military intelligence.

The one that Beta had secretly hoped in her heart-of-hearts would be at her side as they dismantled Bryk's entire network.

Beta had allowed herself to get so lost in her morose thoughts that she didn't realize that Bryk's girlfriend had approached until the other woman slid into the booth on the other side of the table.

"I'll join you in a drink," said the other woman.

She signaled the bartender, a silent man who'd taken the place of Bryk's former bartender and hitman, Jerzego, after Beta had taken him out of play. This new man refused to meet Beta's gaze.

Wise man.

When Bryk's girlfriend looked back at her, Beta narrowed her eyes to mere slits. Doing so gave her the odd impression that she could see the rapid pulse in the other woman's throat and the shaky heat signature of her body.

"I did not say that you could join me," she said, watching that pulse stutter.

"True." Bryk's girlfriend shrugged. She steadied her breathing as she gripped the shot of vodka that the bartender set in front of her. "But perhaps you'd rather be my friend and drink with me than have me tell Bryk that you followed us this afternoon to the planetarium."

Beta remained slouched in her seat. But now it was *her* pulse thrumming. "Be careful," she said before pouring herself more whisky and pinning her gaze on the other woman. "I am not as malleable as Bryk."

"Of course not." Bryk's girlfriend tossed the shot back, closed her eyes for a moment, and then set the empty glass on the scarred wooden table with a soft knock. She held Beta's gaze despite her obvious trembling. "But I think you'll help me find my sister. Bryk has her imprisoned somewhere with other women, in Chorzów, I think. That man at the planetarium today? The one who sat behind us. He's Bratva. He's their caretaker."

Beta kept her expression neutral but focused all of her attention on the other woman. She, like Bryk, had also underestimated his pretty blond girlfriend. The one whose nerves betrayed a slight Russian accent in her voice. The one who was sleeping with the enemy to save her sister.

The one who'd read Beta right.

"What is your name?" asked Beta, sipping Trebitsch.

"Kira."

"Hm. The name of a queen."

Kira looked down. Beta glimpsed a sheen on her eyes before her lids descended.

"What is your sister's name?"

"Katia. Please," said Kira, her hands reflexively reaching for Beta's and then dropping before she could touch them. "She's only fifteen. I can't bear to think about what it's like for her in that awful place."

"I fail to understand what you think that I can do for Katia," said Beta. It was always best to get expectations stated upfront.

Kira shrugged and relaxed. "I've seen the way you protect the servers here. Not just from customers but staff too." She paused, weighing her words before leaning forward and speaking in a low voice. "Beata told me that before, last summer, you helped a woman who could have died from a miscarriage."

Beta's heart hammered in her chest. Her little side gig with the American operative had been contained. Or so she'd thought. How had one of the current servers heard about the woman hemorrhaging in an apartment guarded by several of Bryk's men?

She shrugged, forcing herself to act calm. "One woman. That I found at the hospital." She tossed back the whisky in her glass.

"Yes, but I think you had something to do with that," said Kira, studying her. "More importantly, I think you want to destroy Kacper's business selling women. Why else would you follow him?" She scoffed. "Not because you have ambitions to run that business for him."

And there they'd reached the crux of the matter. Her foolish obsession with crippling Bryk's trafficking business had overridden her objective of finding out who was selling Czech armaments to the Polish crime lord. She could at least protect *that* secret.

"Let us say that I do have a reason to affect his bottom line in that way. How do you expect me to help Katia? I am just one woman."

"*We* are *two* women," said Kira.

"Hm." Beta didn't immediately respond. Instead, she rolled the empty tumbler between her hands. "I perhaps know someone who could help us," she said at last.

Then she set the tumbler carefully on the table and poured another shot before pinning Kira with a steady gaze.

"But first, you will tell me everything you know about your sister, Kacper's business, and that vicious Russian goon guarding the women."

Olivia left the flat she'd rented in the Roman neighborhood of San Giovanni early, blending with the locals who made their way to the metro to commute to work. The neighborhood sat just outside the old city walls, so a few intrepid tourists scattered throughout the mass of Romans on the sidewalk, their telltale colorful clothing and shorts drawing the gaze as much as their propensity to stop and take photos with their smartphones.

She'd stopped at a coffee bar on her route and ordered a morning espresso to drink quickly *al banco*—at the counter—like an Italian when her phone rang. She looked at the screen and frowned. She hadn't seen that number in months.

She answered. "*Ciao, bella.*"

"*Ciao,*" said Anastasia Fiore, an officer with the *Agenzia Informazioni e Sicurezza Esterna,* Italy's version of the CIA. "I am hurt, *cara,* that you did not call me when you arrived in Rome."

Olivia sighed, closing her eyes for a moment before paying the proprietor for the espresso. She turned away from the counter, leaving the potent brew untouched.

"I've been a little busy."

"Indeed. Bringing in one of Imam Alami's men after he attacked your safehouse in Kotor would certainly explain it." Stasia paused and then said, "But, never mind that. I have come to you." This last she said as she walked up behind Olivia.

Olivia swung around, narrowing her eyes as her gaze took in the petite Italian spy, who smiled warmly and ordered a *caffè doppio* and *panino* from the hovering bar owner, handing him cash while murmuring, "*Alla tavola, per favore.*"

Once he'd turned away and began making the double shot, Olivia used the hissing sound of the espresso maker to mask her low-voiced response. "You're awfully well informed for someone not cleared for that information."

Stasia shrugged and nodded toward Olivia's espresso. "You should drink that, *bellisima*, before it gets cold. Let him bring it to you." She tilted her head toward the entrance where small tables could be glimpsed through the open door.

Stasia didn't wait for Olivia's response. Instead, she pivoted and strode outside. Olivia, burning with curiosity and not a little annoyance, followed as the other woman made her way to the farthest table on the sidewalk. The bar owner, carrying a tray with both espressos and a sandwich, brought up the rear of this parade. Once he'd set everything onto the table and nodded at Stasia's murmured *grazie*, he left them alone.

As soon as he had gotten out of listening distance, Olivia said, "Don't even think about taking a bite out of that *panino*."

Stasia grinned. "I bought it for you," she said, waving a hand before sipping her *caffè doppio*. "I thought you might want to offer it to the pregnant woman that you brought with you to Rome. I have found that a full stomach goes a long way toward helping people answer important questions. Plus, you look like you have not been eating well, *cara*. A meal shared builds a great deal of camaraderie, such as the camaraderie we are building now over a *caffè, sì*?"

Olivia ignored the question and asked one of her own. "Were you watching me in Kotor?"

Stasia shook her head, a smile playing around her lips.

Understanding dawned in Olivia. "You were watching Alami."

Stasia nodded. "We have been following the leads on Savik's buyers that we recovered in the Venice raid. Thank you, by the way, for not sharing with your agency the news that we lost a Predator drone in the first place."

"It would have been a poor way to repay your trust in me. And not at all what friends do."

"Better than sharing coffee?" asked Stasia, a glint of amusement in her warm gaze.

Olivia rolled her eyes. Talking to Stasia was going to take some getting used to. "Besides, you covered for me with the CIA."

"Little good it did you," said Stasia. The humor had fled. "Demoting you to housekeeper for the Kotor safehouse is one step above burning you for missions in the field."

Olivia shrugged. "I asked for the placement. I'm not sure I want to continue fieldwork. There will always be terrorists hellbent on blowing up the world."

"And women and children being trafficked," said Stasia, referring to the operation they'd worked together in Venice. "Working a cover at a clinic with immigrants lets you do some good while you figure out your true vocation."

Olivia nodded.

Stasia tilted her head. "And allows you to have a serious relationship with a very handsome French doctor, *sì*?"

Olivia played with her engagement ring. She knew that the sharp-eyed Italian spy had already noted it. "I'm not sure where things stand with Étienne right now. He's already gone to Paris."

Stasia laid her hand over Olivia's hands, stilling their action. When she spoke, her gaze and manner were serious. "That is why, *cara*, you should always have frivolous encounters while operating in the field. It is safer for you, but more importantly, kinder to others. I have never had a serious relationship for this reason."

Olivia held the other woman's gaze. The compassion and understanding she saw there nearly undid her.

She looked away before clearing her throat and continuing. "But I can't leave Merjam to the tender mercies of the CIA, not after our recovery expert lost his whole team in Kotor and Alami escaped. At least the Rome station chief has been willing to let me stay with her while she and her brother Esad are being interrogated."

Stasia nodded gravely. A sudden intuition told Olivia all she needed to know.

"I suspect you had something to do with that."

Stasia shrugged. "I know some people in the Rome office."

"Well, thank you." Olivia paused before returning to business. "Of course, I'll be happy to share whatever I learn about Imam Alami, including whether he has the Predator drone."

"*Grazie*," said Stasia dipping her head.

Olivia's phone rang. She sighed. She hadn't intended to dawdle on her way into the Rome station. Pulling her phone from her purse, she expected to see the number from Greg Hanson, the CIA officer assigned to investigate Alami now that he'd resurfaced with a name and an identifiable network.

It wasn't. It was Alžběta Czerná, the Czech army captain who'd saved Olivia's life last year on a mission in Poland that had gone pear shaped—not a little due to Olivia. Afterwards, they'd gone off the reservation together to rescue a few dozen trafficked teenagers from Kacper Bryk, the leader of a Polish crime syndicate.

Olivia answered. She listened for several long moments, her fingers playing with the spoon next to her now-cold espresso.

After Beta finished, Olivia said, "Prague is lovely this time of year." Then she hung up.

She looked up at Stasia, who watched her like a bright-eyed bird.

"How would you feel about joining me on a little unsanctioned operation to rescue women from the clutches of a Bratva enforcer?"

Stasia studied Olivia for a moment before she smiled widely and warmly. "*Bella*," she said, "Did I not tell you? I have just now received a tip concerning one of Savik's buyers in Prague."

Olivia smiled back at her.

FIVE

Two days later, Stasia wondered what exactly had possessed her to travel to Prague to help an American operative who, by her own admission, intended to engage in an illicit operation that had nothing to do with the CIA, let alone foreign security threats to Italy.

True, Stasia felt a certain debt toward her American cousin, and she always did what she could to repay her debts in the field. It could mean the difference between life and death at the right moment. It was also true that Stasia had had to look the other way against her will more than once on a mission when innocent people had gotten embroiled in the action.

In fact, Stasia's mentor had reprimanded her on her first mission when she'd doubled back to check on a terrified young boy left alone in a dilapidated house. They'd been in Albania tracking a crime ring smuggling heroin from Afghanistan into Italian military bases. He chided her on risking their cloak of invisibility, something vital to their ability to operate inside foreign borders.

Yet here Stasia was walking through the Old Town of Prague, whose very buildings emanated a gothic pall over the sunny June morning, on her way to a meeting with Olivia Markham and an unknown Czech agent to plan an operation to free a woman with no intelligence value for her.

They met at a dark Irish pub named Rocky O'Reillys just off of Wenceslas Square and across from the Hotel Majestic. Stasia wrinkled her nose at the site, wondering if the Czech had chosen it as a means of testing everyone's commitment. If so, she couldn't blame the other woman, who was currently embedded on an official mission with the Polish criminal employing the Bratva enforcer that Olivia had mentioned. Meeting in a popular tourist venue filled with drunken patrons minimized the risk that anyone would overhear them.

Stasia ignored the raucous cheers from the men crowding in front of the numerous big-screen TVs where various sports played. She went to the bar, surreptitiously scanning the crowded room as she did. Prague had many smokers, and most restaurants and bars operated in a haze. She ordered a Czech pilsner, cataloguing the number and kind of threats around her while she waited.

Olivia appeared at her shoulder as she lifted the pilsner for a sip. "We're in the other room," she said, her voice pitched for Stasia's ears. She nodded toward a wide opening in the far wall where another room filled with Irish kitsch could be seen. "Non-smoking, where it's quieter so we can talk."

Stasia nodded and followed the blond agent into the other side of the pub. There a handful of smaller TVs showed various sports on mute, and behind the low hum of voices, Irish music played. Even without her intelligence training, Stasia would have identified the Czech officer they were meeting.

She sat in a corner facing out, her alert gaze taking in every aspect of the pub around them. A bottle of hard liquor sat next to an empty shot glass on the table in front of her. An almost visible air of menace formed a buffer between her table and the others, where pubgoers shifted away from the threat that they sensed in their presence.

Olivia didn't seem to notice the Czech's warning signals. Instead, she walked right up to the table and pulled out a chair, sitting with her own back towards the room.

Stasia followed more slowly, studying the dark-haired woman whose narrowed gaze telegraphed suspicion and hostility. When she arrived, she took a seat to the side of Olivia and closest to an empty table. It was the best she could do to defend from potential threats, but something told her that the greatest threat in Rocky O'Reilly's was the young Czech woman sitting across from her.

Before Olivia could introduce them, a few drunk males entered the non-smoking section from the larger main room, their collective gaze searching until they identified what they were looking for: the women's table.

Stasia groaned inwardly as the group of men, cheering and chattering, jostled their way toward the unsanctioned conclave.

A low hiss from the Czech drew Stasia's startled look. The other woman gripped the whisky bottle with one hand. A short, hooked blade protruded from her other fist like a stainless-steel talon. Her dark eyes gleamed with a feral light. Stasia caught a faint whiff of something acrid, like smoke.

Wrinkling her nose, she shook her head to clear the illusion. *Mi trovo tra l'incudine e il Martello. I find myself between the anvil and the hammer.* She sighed and shifted in her seat, preparing for the ugly scene she knew was about to take place.

Olivia glanced at her, a wry smile acknowledging their situation. "Perhaps you and I can encourage them to find somewhere else to direct their attention before our friend uses stronger methods?"

Stasia glanced between Olivia and the men, who'd arrived, boxing the three of them into the corner. She didn't have to look at the Czech to feel the tension emanating from her.

Dipping her chin, Stasia rose in a graceful movement that snared the male gazes as she'd intended. From the periphery of her vision, she glimpsed Olivia leaning toward the Czech a moment before standing at Stasia's shoulder.

Stasia smiled, letting it light her whole face in effusive warmth. The men, caught off guard, crowded around her. She refrained from dropping her hand into her pocket where she carried a tactical pen. Instead, even as she greeted them, she scanned the men for a hint of anything she could use to divert them toward. There. Several of the men wore Manchester United jerseys.

She glanced at Olivia and winked. Olivia nodded.

"Red Devils, lads?" asked Stasia with a Scouse accent learned while traveling in Liverpool as a child. "Me fella just there"—she waved toward the larger room behind them—"says that youse lads g'wed be right done for now that ol' Sir Alex has retired."

The drunk men turned to stare at the Liverpool fans who watched a recording of a previous match between their rival teams. Stasia knew she had them hooked. It just needed a little push to get the group of men to leave them alone.

"G'on, ask him, lads. While you're at it, ask him about his lad Suárez." Gesturing, she added an eyeroll and dismissive tone to her next words. "Says the Cannibal will chew right through the Red Devils when they meet next."

Anger flared at the name of the popular Liverpool striker, who'd twice been suspended in his career for biting another player, most recently in April. That didn't stop the Liverpool fans from voting him the team's player of the season.

Swearing and seething, the group turned to head back into the pub, their interest in Stasia, Olivia, and the Czech dissipating in the much stronger lure of a brawl with the unsuspecting Liverpool fans. A sole male remained, however, leering at Stasia.

"Your boyfriend's about to get the beatin' of his life," he said, holding a half empty pint glass at an angle that sloshed beer as he spoke. "And you're about to get the best bang of yours." Saying this, he leaned in close and took Stasia's arm before she could step aside, his boozy hot breath washing over her face.

But the Czech caught him by the collar of his shirt with that steel talon she'd held at the ready, her elbow coming around to hammer his jaw even as she pulled him toward her.

As he crumpled to his knees, the pint glass still clutched in his hand, she stepped to the side and dragged his forehead into the table's edge. He slid all the way to the floor.

Stasia blinked at the speed and precision of the attack. Not to mention the explosive violence.

Olivia looked down at the unconscious Brit. "I suggest we take our meeting elsewhere before the whole place erupts into a brawl." She glanced at the Czech. "Though I doubt it would last long, it would make it hard to talk about why we're really here."

They formed into a wedge behind Olivia, who led them out of the secondary entrance to the street where tourists crowded the sidewalk in front of the hotel. Stasia's antennae caught the excited chatter from the pub patrons who'd witnessed the event. Laughter reassured her. No one was likely to complain or report them.

Olivia headed toward Wenceslas Square, a long, bustling commercial district with Stasia at her side. The Czech trailed them. Stasia could hear the repeated soft *snick* of the small knife she carried, likely an Indonesian karambit given the shape of its blade. Something told Stasia that it wasn't nerves that caused the other woman to open and close it over and over.

"Museum, McDonald's or shopping?" asked Olivia as she strode.

"None," said the Czech, speaking for the first time in Stasia's hearing. She continually scanned the environment for threats.

Olivia threw an affectionate look over her shoulder. "Your apartment then?" At the Czech's scowl, she laughed. "Shopping it is. Come, I want to see that statue by your relative, David Černý."

The scowl deepened, but the other woman said nothing. Given her faded jeans and T-shirt, it seemed clear that she disdained clothes shopping despite having the height and build that would make her the envy of runway models in Milan.

Stasia tucked this insight into her growing profile of the mysterious third woman.

Olivia led them along the wide sidewalk, skillfully weaving among the slow-moving tourists toward a store-size opening nearly hidden between the Hotel Rokoko and a sporting goods store. The sign over the opening read "Pasáž Rokoko."

They walked inside the passage, which led them past retail shops to a set of steps up to another passage, the Lucerna Passage, that felt more like a tunnel with its arched ceiling and lighted sign cases. It opened up to a tiled rotunda with a statue of a man riding an upside-down horse hanging from a windowed dome. Steps led to a level below and a level above. Beyond the rotunda, more shops lined an arcade leading back outside.

They stopped to admire the irreverent statue of St. Wenceslas while people, tourists and locals seeking an air-conditioned shortcut, streamed past.

Olivia turned to the Czech. "You're much better with that karambit than I ever hope to be. It belongs in your hands."

"It was a gift."

Olivia smiled. "Let's call it a loan that I'm now returning."

The dark-haired woman dipped her chin.

Stasia's patience finally frayed to nothing. Throwing her hand up, she said, "*Santo cielo!* I could have handled that boor myself without leaving him on the floor unconscious." She glared at the Czech. "We could have been arrested, which I do not have to tell you would not help us. Anyone risking exposure on my operations gets yanked out of the field."

The Czech stiffened and bared her teeth at Stasia, whose own hackles rose in response.

Looking back and forth between them, Olivia sighed and fingered her pendant, a small silver disc that Stasia recognized as a saint's medal. Stasia had the odd impression that the American spy said a prayer for help.

Then Olivia turned, smiled at Stasia, and said, "Stasia Fiore, meet Beta Czerná. Let's get a coffee at the Costa Coffee"—here she gestured with her chin toward the arcade—"and discuss how Beta is going to take point on this operation."

Stasia recognized the subtle voice of command and the bare emphasis on the word *this* and shifted, folding her arms.

"I have yet to be convinced that this *is* an operation," she said. "And not some sort of gamble with unknown and unpredictable players."

"So, a trial by fire?" asked Olivia, alluding to Stasia's impromptu decision to include her on an AISE mission taking down a Serbian arms dealer.

The one that went hot, and Stasia ended up killing the Serb's son as he strangled Olivia.

Stasia had the grace to flush. But she refused to back down. She'd come here out of a sense of debt to Olivia and because she'd gotten a taste for rescuing trafficking victims that left her deeply dissatisfied with the more indirect and opaque game of intelligence gathering—especially on a mission to recover a Predator drone her government should never have lost. Nevertheless, she wasn't sure this little rogue operation would be worth the risks.

"I will drink a coffee with you and listen to your proposal." She let a tone of warning enter her words to signal that listening was all that she agreed to do. "But *not* at Costa Coffee. I have a better place where everyone will have to be on their best behavior."

She left unsaid that her choice of venue upped the risk of exposure for anyone unable to behave professionally. Both Olivia and Beta either understood that or they didn't. In that case, the nascent team would be stillborn there.

Thirty minutes later, they found themselves across the Vltava River in the Malá Strana neighborhood at the Café Savoy, a historic café renovated a decade before in a classic Viennese Art Nouveau style. Despite not having reservations, they'd been seated quickly at a table on the upper gallery. Stasia clearly knew someone at the popular coffee shop.

Olivia gripped her impatience and waited for their coffees to arrive. She'd ordered an Americano with milk and lightly sweetened, while Stasia had chosen a macchiato. Beta, to her surprise, had ordered the Café au lait Savoy, sweetened with Valrhona chocolate and cinnamon. Apparently, the taciturn Czech had a sweet tooth. She'd also relaxed, something that Olivia only recognized after having spent hours working with her—and the karambit stayed hidden. Olivia sent up a silent prayer that Stasia's choice would reset their team introduction.

At last, the coffees and a pastry for Beta had been delivered. Olivia ignored hers to get down to brass tacks.

She looked at Stasia. "Despite your qualms, I have perfect confidence in Beta. She saved my life and risked her cover after I did something stupid." Hearing Stasia's sharp intake of breath, she moved quickly on. "Whatever we do, we must not risk Beta's cover with Kacper Bryk. But I think we can leverage that cover and get rid of his Bratva goon at the same time."

Beta leaned back in her chair, her arms crossed despite the untouched *café au lait* and *pain au chocolat* in front of her. She ignored Stasia to speak to Olivia. "I have a complication. My investigation has been stymied now that Bryk has mobile headquarters."

"Mobile headquarters?" asked Olivia, frowning. "You mean he conducts business from his car?" She whistled. "That's one way to compartmentalize operations."

Beta nodded. "No one but his driver rides with him. And a security team sweeps his vehicle daily to ensure that no one plants a listening device or tracker."

"Can you gain physical access to his cellphone?" asked Stasia, sounding intrigued.

Thank God thought Olivia.

Then Stasia ruined it by adding, "Of course, that would require finesse, not combat skills."

Beta said nothing, simply turning her impassive gaze to the Italian operative and then looking back at Olivia. "Bryk has a separate cellphone for scheduling meetings that he leaves in the van. His primary cellphone he keeps locked up in his office at The Wild Stallion when he conducts business off site."

Olivia thought for a moment as she tested her instinct about this news. As far as she could tell, her initial reaction had legs.

She looked at both women. "That makes our plan perfect."

Stasia raised an eyebrow and tilted her head. "And what exactly is our plan?" She raised her macchiato and sipped.

"We grab the Bratva enforcer and interrogate him. He's likely the only one who knows where the victims are being kept. Given Bryk's busy schedule, I'd say we probably have a good 48 hours to get the information out of him before Bryk notices he's missing."

Beta sat forward, her gaze intent. "I have a way to divert Bryk's attention for a few days."

Stasia frowned as she set her cup down. "That will not work, *cara*. Those men are extremely loyal. And they take punishment in service of their captains as a reward. He will tell us nothing, not even if we try to seduce him."

"That's where Beta comes in," said Olivia, grinning at Beta. "Whose skills of persuasion run in a different direction."

Beta shocked Olivia by smiling back.

Stasia looked between both of them. "What am I missing? You said that we must not risk Beta's cover. How are we going to use her?"

"She will also be interrogated."

Stasia blinked as she processed this news. "Ah," she said as she worked through Olivia's proposed scenario. "I see. She will gain his trust as another member of Bryk's organization, perhaps playing on the fact that they are both loyal yet isolated. They must stick together against their interlocuters."

She pursed her lips as she studied Beta. "It could work. But he might test you. Are you afraid to be in such close proximity with an undoubtedly violent Russian criminal?"

For answer, Beta showed Stasia the karambit, which appeared as if by magic in her right hand. Without speaking, she focused on the other woman as she demonstrated opening and closing the wicked little tactical knife, all while passing it between both hands with lightning speed. And without once looking away.

She finished by hooking the cloth napkin next to her plate and lifting it in a single motion to reveal the undamaged table beneath.

Stasia shook her head. "Of course not. Why did I ask?" She looked back at Olivia. "And what will be our roles in this operation?"

"Ah, well, we get to play ourselves," said Olivia, smiling again. "An Italian foreign intelligence officer working with an American CIA officer to find a stolen Predator drone. Our investigation has led us to Bryk's syndicate, and we've scooped up vulnerable players to squeeze."

Stasia looked startled and then laughed. "Ah, *bella*, you have extended my ploy very cleverly! Let us hope that it backstops us both with our agencies if our activities come to light." She tilted her head. "Which one of us will play good cop as you Americans say?"

"I should think that would be obvious: you," said Olivia. "I'll play unhinged. I have some angst that I need to get out anyway, given everything that's going on."

Stasia, whose sympathetic gaze told Olivia that she understood her allusion, nodded and finished her macchiato. She stood. "Then I suggest that we adjourn our meeting so that I may check in with my local field office to help sell this play."

She looked at Beta. "I trust you can supply an appropriate location. I will supply my own gear. Olivia, text me when you are ready to head to Katowice."

"Copy that. I want to check in with a friend of mine in Prague, so give me a few hours. We can grab dinner later to go over logistics and tactics once we know more specifics."

Stasia left them, stopping by the counter on the first floor to speak with a tall, dignified man wearing a dark gray suit. The subtle blush on her cheeks and her hand on his forearm told Olivia all she needed to know.

"Where did you find her?" asked Beta once Stasia left the Café Savoy. She had devoured the pastry after Stasia left the table, and now sat licking her fingers clean. "She is more dangerous than she likes to pretend."

Olivia, who'd been lost thinking about Étienne for a moment, brought her gaze and her attention back to her friend.

"Of course she is," she said, tasting her Americano at last. It was tepid. She scrunched her nose and sipped again.

Beta speared her with a gaze every bit as pointed as her hidden karambit. "You trust her?"

"With my life," said Olivia. "Which she has already saved. Though in her case, she was the one who put me in danger, so she will be extra motivated to have my back."

"Good," said Beta, clearly satisfied. "Because Bryk has moved on from buying obsolete Czech arms to the latest generation of combat weaponry. I intend to use my persuasive skills to turn the Bratva enforcer into a double agent. He will lead me to Bryk's supplier."

Six

The next morning, the three operatives met at the abandoned train depot in the center of Katowice, the site that Beta had identified as ideal for interrogating Bryk's Russian enforcer. Olivia and Stasia, who'd shared a hotel room the night before, arrived together to find Beta leaning against a small outbuilding at the edge of the weed-choked compound of derelict, graffiti-scrawled buildings. The desolate sight gave Olivia the creeps.

"Nice digs," she said as she and Stasia approached the Czech. They both carried a large duffel bag with their favorite tools of the trade. "Are you sure this place is deserted? The amount of tagging"—here she gestured toward the vertical surfaces around them with their multi-colored, spray-painted letters and artwork—"suggests that this place is the favorite hangout of the local urban-artist population."

Beta shrugged. "It is one of many. I will leave it to you two to shoo any stragglers away." She turned to lead them around the corner to the door.

Stasia wrinkled her nose as she and Olivia fell into step behind Beta. "The smell here is atrocious! Something has crawled under the foundation and died. My head already aches."

Olivia looked in sympathy over her shoulder at the petite Italian spy. "I have some Vaseline that I scented with rose oil. It doesn't completely block bad smells, but it mutes them enough for me to concentrate. I can share."

"*Grazie*," said Stasia as she tugged the strap of her duffel bag higher on her shoulder.

The entry door of the outbuilding led into a main room about 40 square meters in size with a single, dirty window. On the opposite wall, another door led to a windowless back room, perhaps a former storage area given the detritus still there, of roughly 15 square meters. As for the main room, Beta had already brought in a small table and chairs along with a portable generator so that they'd have lights and fan in the stuffy space.

Olivia, setting her bag on the smooth concrete floor, noted that the laconic Czech had tidied up as well, removing the garbage and sweeping the dirt, cobwebs, and animal spoor out. From what she'd seen on their trek through the depot grounds, Beta must have also cleared used condoms and needles and empty liquor bottles. Alone. There was no operational support team to do it for them.

Dusty and dim it might be, but she and Stasia would be much more comfortable than either Beta or the Bratva enforcer during the interrogation. They would be confined in the hot, filthy back room. It was still early, yet sweat already dampened Olivia's underarms.

"It must have taken you hours to clean up," said Olivia, letting gratitude color her voice. "Thanks for doing it." She bent to rummage in her bag for the scented Vaseline to loan to Stasia.

Stasia, who'd been studying their workspace, turned to accept the tub of petroleum jelly. As she opened the lid, she said, "Indeed, you have done a better job than an AISE team."

Beta shrugged a shoulder as she moved away from them to turn on the tall fan standing in a corner. "I did what was necessary to sell your cover story."

Despite her nonchalance, Olivia sensed that Beta was pleased with their acknowledgment. She let out a soundless sigh. Creating a team in the wild was proving more challenging than she might have guessed.

They'd gone over their roles and discussed tactics once they held Bryk's man when they addressed the heart of the matter: how to get a loyal and suspicious Bratva member under their control in the first place. Even though Beta had managed to narrow the sites where the Russian kept the trafficked victims to locations in Chorzów, she'd failed to nail down how frequently he moved them or how often he and Bryk communicated. They also discussed viable locations from which to snatch the Russian.

Olivia turned to Beta. "Given the constraints, we have to get access to Bryk's cellphone in his van. It's the only way to contact the Bratva caretaker. Stasia and I can do it if you can guarantee he'll be occupied elsewhere long enough for us to manage."

"I have a better idea," said a woman from the doorway behind them. "I can get the phone when Kacper takes me to lunch today."

Olivia and Stasia shifted in their seats in unison, each aiming a weapon at the stranger.

Beta, leaning against a wall with her arms and ankles crossed said, "This is Kira. Her fifteen-year-old sister Katia came to Poland looking for her. Bryk promised Katia a modeling job. I promised to help Katia. Kira knows that you are my friends."

To Beta's credit, the last came out naturally.

"Bryk has her? Are you sure?" asked Olivia even as Stasia made an exasperated sound and shifted in her seat.

The next few minutes were going to be tricky indeed. It was for sure that Kira had no idea who they really were. Olivia slipped her weapon back into its shoulder holster. Next to her, Stasia set her own gun onto the table.

Kira answered instead. "I found her photo with other photos in a folder in his desk."

Everyone looked at her.

"What in the world were you doing searching his desk?" asked Olivia. "If he caught you, you'd be lucky if he sold you. More likely, he'd kill you and show your body to her."

Kira's chin rose. When she answered, she sounded defiant. "He did not catch me. I pretended to look for him in his office when I knew that he was not there. Also, he does not know that Katia is my sister."

"I do not like this," said Stasia, sounding deeply unhappy. "It is never a good idea to use an untrained civilian in an operation, especially one in such a precarious position."

Kira lasered her gaze on Stasia. "I will do anything for my sister. Anything. Including sleep with the man who imprisons her," she said. A world of meaning filled her statement.

Olivia looked at Beta. "This is how you planned to get Bryk out of town for a few days."

Beta nodded. She said nothing, just watched Olivia with her intense dark-gray eyes.

Olivia looked at Stasia, who frowned.

"It is not my operation," she said.

"No, it isn't," said Olivia. "But I'm sure that Beta values your opinion. I know I do. And we certainly can't pull this operation off without you."

Stasia sighed and looked at Kira. "Are you sure that you can get access to this phone? Have you even seen it?"

Kira nodded. "He keeps it in a built-in cabinet in the side panel."

Stasia persisted. "And you think that you can get your hands on it without Bryk being aware that you have?"

Kira's spine straightened. "I *know* that I can." She looked at Stasia. "I know things that can help you. Such as that the man you seek has a tattoo of a polar wolf on his back."

As the young woman spoke, Olivia was reminded of Marina Orlova, the young Russian embassy employee who'd dared to alert the CIA to a nuclear deal unfolding between a Russian general and an associate of Bryk's. A presentiment washed through her, but Olivia didn't know whether it was for Kira or Marina.

Before she could speak, Stasia said, "Bryk likely shuts off this phone before he leaves the vehicle. If you can power it up after he puts it in the cabinet, his instinct will be to think that he forgot to shut it down when he takes it out again."

Stasia looked at Olivia. "I still do not like it, but that will be the safest and fastest thing for her to do."

"How will that help if he's not using it?" asked Kira, puzzled.

Olivia looked at the other two operatives before answering the young woman.

She cleared her throat. "Ah, um, there are tools that will allow us to locate the cellphone signal and access the phone itself remotely. That will help us find your sister," she said. She looked at Beta, "That is, if Beta's other *friends* will help us out."

Beta grinned fiercely. "My friends Andrej and Eliska have such a tool. And they owe me."

After Kira left, escorted by Beta who would return to The Wild Stallion where she worked as Bryk's manager, Stasia and Olivia familiarized themselves with the grounds of the former locomotive depot before concentrating on the dilapidated building.

By midday they'd installed Wi-Fi cameras on the exterior of the building to alert them to activity outside. For the interrogation room itself, they placed tiny wireless FM transmitters that Stasia had procured from an Israeli outfitter in unlikely places: a gouged hole in one wall, inside a defunct light fixture dangling from the ceiling, and on top of a rusted metal cabinet. They also confirmed the integrity of the walls and scoured the room to ensure that Beta had left nothing behind that could be used as a weapon.

Stasia, who wore black gloves, dropped an oily bit of rag on the floor with a sound of disgust. She sighed and stretched her back. "This is pointless. He does not need a weapon beyond his hands to kill her."

Olivia, who'd carefully sifted through a pile of rotting lumber to check for splinters large enough to gouge an eye or puncture an artery, exhaled and stood upright. "*She* won't be unarmed. As long as he's not frisking her, she can defend herself until one of us gets here. That reminds me, which shift do you want?"

"Hm," said Stasia, stripping off her gloves as she returned to the main room. "I think that I should go first. Then we can argue over jurisdiction and tactics in front of him before you interrogate him. He must believe that we are who we say we are and that Bryk has been targeted. He will be desperate to escape to move the victims."

Olivia nodded, grabbing a bottle of water from the soft-sided cooler in the corner, opening it, and drinking it half down. "I've never been in charge of an interrogation before," she said. "My old team leader handled them."

Stasia shrugged before pulling her own water bottle from the cooler. "You have good instincts. Just remember that the goal is to push him to trust Beta. Of course, all of this depends on Kira's success gaining access to Bryk's cellphone."

Olivia laughed wryly. "It's funny. I'm not even an active field agent, and I'm conducting an interrogation."

She sat down and powered up the laptop to finish setting up the security cameras and wireless transmitters.

As she logged in, she said, "Just so you know, I'm also uncomfortable about using Kira. She reminds me of a young Russian I recruited as an asset last year in Prague—full of passion and drive. She got us some very valuable intel. It's how I met Beta."

When Stasia didn't respond, Olivia looked up to see the other intelligence officer watching her with her arms folded.

"What?" she asked.

Stasia lifted a shoulder. "It sounds like you are describing yourself."

"Perhaps," said Olivia. "But I've learned the hard way that not everyone at the CIA has my best interests at heart. And that I need partners who have my back when the going gets tough."

"Did you learn something from this former asset yesterday that worries you?"

Of course. Stasia had put two and two together.

Olivia hesitated for only a moment. If she trusted Stasia enough to work on an unsanctioned operation, she could certainly trust her with the misgivings she had over Marina's news.

"She told me that she'd learned more about this Polish arms broker named Bogdi Król that she thought the CIA would be interested in.

When I warned her that she hadn't been trained for fieldwork, she just laughed. She said that working with me had inspired her. She also said she'd reached out to the Prague station and gotten a new handler, but she was pretty coy about it."

Just then their cellphones vibrated with simultaneous notifications. Both of them checked to see that Beta had texted them with confirmation that her contacts in Czech military intelligence had agreed to track Bryk's secure cellphone. In fact, her friends would be in Katowice later that day with an IMSI catcher, known colloquially in the U.S. as a stingray. Best case scenario: Olivia and her partners would be able to spoof a text to the Bratva caretaker before nightfall.

"Okay," said Olivia, finalizing the checks on their surveillance equipment. She'd set the system to relay any notifications of incursions to their cellphones. "Time to scout out the potential sites to grab Mr. Bratva Goon."

Stasia laughed as she picked up a leather satchel and slung it over her shoulder. "Ivan Ivanov is what AISE calls Russians of interest."

They spent the rest of the day visiting locations that Beta had pre-selected for them: Club Pomarańcza, one of the largest nightclubs in the region, and Silesia Park, a large piece of reclaimed industrial land that straddled the border of Katowice and Chorzów. Besides the planetarium, which Beta had told them that Bryk had already used to meet his Russian subordinate, there was an amusement park, a zoo, a cable car, a rose garden, and a central forest crisscrossed by roads, alleys, and endless paths with benches.

Olivia and Stasia had returned to the depot compound to discuss and rank their options when Beta called early that evening. Olivia put her on speakerphone.

"I have good news and bad news," she said without preamble. "The good news is that my friends will have the phone's IMSI and potential targets soon."

"What's the bad news?" asked Olivia, looking at Stasia, who was in the middle of eating pierogi slathered in sour cream. It was their first actual meal of the day.

"Something has spooked Bryk. He has ordered extra security for The Wild Stallion and forbidden his closest subordinates to leave."

"That includes you," said Olivia. Now the Italian operative's keen gaze held hers.

"Yes." Noise from Beta's environment filtered over the open line. From the acoustics, it sounded like someone had just opened a door into a restroom.

"You aren't alone now, are you?" asked Olivia.

"No" came the terse reply.

Olivia, her gaze still on Stasia's in an effort to gauge the other operative's response, said, "Okay, just listen. We can work around that. You keep an eye on Bryk while we handle Ivan."

Before Beta could answer, Stasia said, "The timing is odd." She set her fork carefully on the plastic with which they'd covered the table. "Are you certain that Bryk suspects nothing?"

There was a long moment of silence. The sound of running water followed a toilet flush. A moment later, chatter and music preceded a sharp cessation of noise.

"I can say nothing for certain," said Beta at last, "but if I had to guess, it has something to do with whoever supplied the latest generation of Skorpion submachine guns to him. Kira said that he took a call this afternoon before he ordered his men to move the weapons from his warehouse."

"Ah, the day job," said Olivia, feeling relief.

At this point, Stasia interjected, "Perhaps now is not a good time to risk grabbing Ivan. In my experience, when a crime boss's paranoia spikes in one part of his operation, it spills over into other parts."

"He's going to be distracted. That's good for our little mission," said Olivia.

"Better this than putting Kira into more danger," said Beta. "In *my* experience, Bryk likes to cull liabilities when threatened."

"Would he kill his stock?" asked Stasia, sounding shocked.

"Yes."

Before either Olivia or Stasia could speak, Beta went on, "One moment. I have a text from my friends. You must decide now if you will continue."

"Or what?" asked Olivia without considering her answer. "Leave you to deal with Bryk *and* his Bratva muscle alone? Forget it, Beta. I'm all in. Text me their numbers."

Stasia sat back in her chair. "And I will not leave Olivia to deal alone with a violent criminal who was incarcerated in one of the worst prisons in Russia."

When Olivia shot the Italian operative a startled glance, she shrugged. "That polar-wolf tattoo Kira mentioned? It means that our target somehow escaped a life sentence in a maximum-security site in the Arctic."

Silence reigned for a moment before Beta broke it.

When she spoke, her voice had lost its sharp edge. "Thank you." She paused a moment before saying, "I will discard this phone once we end our call. Send me confirmation via the backup method I gave you once you have him."

And then the line went dead.

Unfortunately for Olivia and Stasia, Beta's Czech military intelligence contacts had been unable to pinpoint the exact number for the Bratva contact. Instead, they'd sent five possibilities.

"What do we do?" asked Olivia. "We can't just send them all texts to meet."

Stasia smiled, a mischievous glint in her eyes. "No, but we can call them. They can't all be Russian, can they?"

Olivia grinned back. "I like the way you think. Okay, how many do you want to call?"

Stasia pulled out the burner phone that she'd already activated for this mission. "I can handle this. You go over the locations we scouted today and determine the best one for only two of us."

"Copy that."

Half an hour later, Stasia had Ivan's number. And Olivia had a location and a plan. Beta's friends would intercept any texts to Bryk's actual phone so that he'd never know that anyone had hijacked his number and contacted his minion.

"I think our best bet is to set the meet at Club Pomarańcza. It's closer to home for Bryk, which fits for a last-minute night meeting. And it's busy enough that it makes sense that Bryk might risk exposure."

"Plus, you look stunning in evening wear."

At twenty past midnight, Olivia stood by their rental car, its trunk open, waiting for the Russian, whom Beta and Kira had described to them. Despite not having a photo of him, the deadly criminal wasn't hard to identify when he arrived: his malicious, saturnine features drew her alert gaze. That, and Olivia identified the snake coiled through the empty eye socket of a skull tattooed on his exposed shoulder. He'd been sentenced to life in prison, and yet here he walked, free, through the parking lot of a Polish dance club.

As he approached the car, Olivia began her faux-drunken schtick, weaving and stumbling as she pretended to search for something in the trunk, waggling her rear enticingly. Once he came close enough, the plan was for Olivia to stun him with a stun gun and shove him into the trunk of the rental car, binding and sedating him before driving to their temporary interrogation site.

But it never happened.

Instead, Olivia's St. Michael medal heated against her chest an instant before something whispered in the air next to her—then embedded in the trunk lid.

Swiveling, she raised the compact CZ P-10 pistol she'd left ready on the floor of the trunk.

Beta stood fifteen meters away with a gun raised in a two-handed grip as she stared at Olivia through its sights. Behind her, Kacper Bryk and a squad of tough-looking men watched them closely. From her peripheral vision, she glimpsed Bryk's Bratva minion swerve and then, throwing a last glance at his boss, jog away.

"We meet again, *Dido*," said Bryk, a silver cap on his teeth glinting in the fluorescent light of the nearby lamppost. "But this time, you don't have your large friend with you, do you? You know the one. The American soldier who pretended to be a Nigerian buyer and then stole a nuclear detonator from me."

SEVEN

If Olivia had a CIA SOG team to extract her, she'd risk being taken rather than engaging in a firefight in a public parking lot.

She didn't have a CIA SOG team.

In fact, her only help had been effectively halved now that Beta stood across from them pointing a weapon at her.

Or had it? There was nothing in particular in the Czech officer's stance and expression to signal that she was anything but ready to shoot them. But Olivia had to trust her new friends. Both of them.

"That's funny you should say that," she said to Bryk without lowering her own weapon, which was trained on him. "Because I have a lot of friends who have my back." *Please let them get my meaning*, she prayed. "In fact, there's a sniper trained on you right now."

Bryk started to laugh. Beta looked over her shoulder at him.

"You do," she said matter-of-factly.

Bryk's laughter stopped. He looked down to see the little red dot dancing on his chest. It moved to his forehead.

"It's on your forehead now," said Beta helpfully.

Bryk's cold gaze burned the air between him and Olivia.

"Stay in my country," he said through clenched teeth, "and I will hunt you down. You and anyone you have working with you."

"Yeah, yeah," said Olivia in a steady voice though her heart raced. "And my little dog, too. I've already seen that kid's movie, Bryk, and it's boring."

Just then, Olivia glimpsed a couple coming toward them from the corner of her eye. They walked on a trajectory that would take them through the middle of the standoff. A willowy blonde, her arm tucked inside that of a massive male who seemed familiar to Olivia, laughed. The dulcet sound dispelled the tension between Olivia and her antagonists. Bryk and the tough-looking men with him glanced toward the couple.

Beta, however, kept her gaze on Olivia. She blinked twice, slowly. Not exactly Morse code, but Olivia got it.

Dipping her chin in acknowledgment, Olivia fired a few rounds at the group, deliberately aiming long and wide. They scattered, each man pulling his own weapon. Beta fired in return, her own shots hitting the pavement next to the rental car, sparks flashing.

A damn fine show of precise marksmanship, missing Olivia on purpose. At the same time, the giant growled and the blonde at his side yelped in surprise. They ducked behind a parked car as Stasia shot two of Bryk's men from her concealed overwatch position.

The next few seconds descended into chaos as Bryk and his remaining men raced behind nearby cars and began shooting at Olivia. Stasia covered her as she slammed the car's trunk closed and dashed around to the driver's side. The gunfire stopped abruptly, allowing Olivia to open the car door and slide in. Starting the car, she shifted into reverse and stomped on the gas, propelling the car down the lane between parked vehicles.

Olivia raced around the club to the pickup point that she and Stasia had set prior to the meet, expecting the Poles to pursue her. But as she waited for Stasia, who ran up to the passenger side of the car two minutes later and jumped into the backseat with her long gun and ammo bag, no vehicles came barreling toward them. Olivia had already started accelerating before Stasia pulled the door shut.

They dumped the car in Bytom, a small city seven kilometers northwest of Katowice, before making their way back to the abandoned locomotive depot grounds. It was nearing sunrise before they crept through the weeds to the outbuilding they'd prepped for their target.

Beta waited for them inside the darkened building.

"Please tell me you got him," said Olivia, as she dropped her bag on the floor and sank into a chair. She wished she had a stiff drink, a hot meal, and a scented bath, in no particular order.

Meanwhile, Stasia quietly settled her gear next to the table and sat down, sighing. She pulled the band off her ponytail and shook her head to release her wavy, caramel-blond hair.

"We did," said Beta. "My friends sat on his apartment until he returned from Club Pomarańcza to be sure."

"Did they also get inside?" asked Stasia, sounding tired, as she rummaged around inside the bag at her feet. She left unstated the rest of the question: *did they plant bugs?*

Beta looked at her. In the early-morning gloom, Olivia thought she saw the glitter of contempt in her gaze.

"Of course" was all she said, however.

Olivia sighed and stretched her arms over her head. It had been a long twenty-four hours, and they still had work to do.

She dropped her arms, sighing again. "We don't have any time to waste. Bryk will focus on the higher-value targets in his contacts as we intended, but the clock's ticking on when he'll call Ivan and tell him to move the women."

"And children," said Beta. "Boys and girls." Her flat tone conveyed a universe of meaning.

It injected renewed urgency into Olivia's flagging spirit. "Well, then, let's get the show on the road," she said. "Beta, I think it's best if you're already here waiting for him. Seeing you will soften his resistance faster."

Beta nodded.

Stasia stood as she lifted the strap of her duffel bag to her shoulder, apparently also rejuvenated. "*Che Dio vi ascolti.*" *May God hear you.*

"Indeed," said Olivia, touching the tip of her finger to her St. Michael medal as she too stood. She checked the clip in her weapon. "Give us a couple of hours. I need more practical clothing and some food before I tackle a Bratva foot soldier. Oh, and Beta"—she reached into her duffel bag and pulled out the karambit—"don't forget this." She tossed it to the other woman.

Beta snatched the closed knife from the air like a bird of prey hunting for a field mouse. She grinned a feral grin. "I would not dream of it."

Less than two hours later, Olivia and Stasia waited in a rental car outside the Russian's apartment in the cool early morning. Olivia had donned a navy suit with a crisp white shirt, pulling her hair back into a neat low ponytail and covering her eyes with brown-gradient navigator sunglasses. Stasia wore tailored black slacks, a white silk shirt, and leather loafers. They needed to convey smooth professionalism and unquestioned authority.

As they'd suspected, Bryk's caretaker had ditched his cellphone after the aborted meeting. Andrej and Eliska, Beta's contacts with Czech military intelligence, had waited outside the Russian's apartment until Olivia and Stasia arrived. They confirmed that he was still inside, but it was only a matter of time before he'd be on the move.

What no one said aloud was that all of their work might be for nothing if Bryk had issued a standing order to kill the women and children if there was trouble. And no one knew where Ivan had been during the hour and a half between the club and his apartment.

"Your friend has astounding marksmanship," said Stasia, her gaze glued to the front door of the target's apartment. "Either that, or you are very fortunate."

Olivia laughed. "I *am* very lucky, but no, she's just that good. I'm just impressed with her throwing that vicious little karambit at that distance and hitting the car. It's not exactly a throwing knife." She looked over at Stasia. "I'd say your sharpshooting skills are equally high caliber. Bryk's men scattered like popcorn popping. Well, except the two you wounded. *That's* some fine targeting there."

Stasia shrugged without looking back at her. "My grandfather, uncles, and father are all *carabinieri*. I learned to shoot a pistol before I learned to drive."

The target's apartment door opened. A tall man, around two meters, came out. He had on a charcoal gray T-shirt with a satiny silver jacket and acid-washed jeans. Even without seeing the copious tattoos, Olivia would have recognized the flat stare and the small scar bisecting his left eyebrow.

"Showtime," she said.

"*In bocca al lupo,*" murmured Stasia.

Olivia recognized the familiar Italian idiom. It was eerily apropos. They were heading into the mouth of the wolf.

A polar wolf to be exact.

Olivia and Stasia brought their quarry, drugged and wearing flexi-cuffs on wrists behind his back, to their interrogation site where they dumped him in the dim, airless room. A small animal had gotten into the room overnight. Now it smelled of urine in addition to the stink of putrefaction from the dead animal under the building's foundation. Olivia's heart twisted for Beta, sitting on the floor while leaning against a wall, her upper lip swollen and covered with crusty dried blood. She'd hated striking the other woman so hard that her head had snapped on her slender neck, but it had had to be done.

Please don't let it all be for nothing, she prayed into the silence. *Don't let it be too late.*

The one thing that they had in their favor was the odds. The Polish crime boss would be reluctant to accept that the Americans and Italians had dragged in a Russian underling in charge of sex slaves to squeeze for information.

Not when his truck loaded with Skorpion submachine guns had been hijacked last night.

Olivia glanced at Beta as she prodded the woozy Russian with a stun gun to his upper back.

The Czech officer's quick thinking and daring theft after Bryk had gone on lockdown gave them a fighting chance to recover Katia and the other victims. She'd left Olivia and Stasia a message confirming her success diverting Bryk's attention: *vlaje falešná vlajka. A false flag flies.*

They dropped the Bratva enforcer in a corner opposite Beta. He groaned but didn't fully come around, which was fine by Olivia. He could stew in captivity for a few hours.

Then they returned to their post in the room outside to listen to the audio captured by the FM transmitters that they'd hidden earlier. It remained maddeningly quiet.

Olivia sighed, removed her sunglasses, and ran her fingers through her hair. That's when she noticed a large brown-paper envelope, the kind sealed with cord, lying among the haphazard paperwork on the table. She pulled the envelope to her and opened it. She could feel Stasia's curious gaze on her.

"It's a call log with some of the calls highlighted," she said, flipping through the documents to a stack of photos. "And surveillance photos of Bryk. Beta must have gotten it from Andrej."

Olivia shoved the documents back into the envelope and forgot about them.

After an hour in which the only sound came from some rodent in the far corner of the room, she stood and said, "Let's move this along."

"As you wish," said Stasia, rising also and taking up her Benelli Nova tactical shotgun.

Olivia had the odd feeling that there had been communication in the room that was disrupted by their appearance, even though the sensitive transmitters had caught nothing.

Interesting.

She strode to Bryk's underling and nudged him, hard, with the toe of her boot.

"Wakey, wakey," she said in a mock cheerful tone.

Stasia took up a post on the other side of the man, holding the Nova in a ready position.

The Russian's eyes opened to reveal a deep malevolence that would have terrified most people he turned it against, including the women and children he guarded. In Olivia's case, it ignited fury—fury that erupted as he deliberately sneered and spat at her. She kicked him in the ribs, careful not to injure his kidney despite the volcanic heat that scalded her chest.

"Now, now," she said in Russian, her voice lowering into a dangerous whisper as she removed her sunglasses. "I wouldn't do that again if I were you." She folded the eyewear and held it casually in her hand.

She sensed more than saw Stasia's shock at her transformation. She ignored it.

Tilting her head toward Beta, she said, "Just ask your colleague how understanding I can be when you fail to show me the respect that I am due."

The Russian's gaze followed hers. Olivia read recognition in it. Nevertheless, he shrugged.

"I am no little girl to fear you. I have taken more than you can possibly give. I have given more than you can imagine. I will deliver more than you can take, that I promise you." He said this with cold matter-of-factness.

Olivia didn't back down. It would be fatal to do so now. Instead, she crouched to eye level with the Russian and, holding his gaze, throat punched him with the hand still holding the sunglasses.

Leaning forward, she spoke in a low voice into his ear as he gagged. "I think you'll find that my imagination more than suffices, comrade."

Stasia shifted, drawing both their gazes. Now she held the combat weapon across her chest. She wore a slight frown.

"We need him to cooperate," she said to Olivia in English, her Italian accent prominent. "He will not be able to tell us what we need to know if his throat swells shut."

Olivia looked up at her. "Be my guest," she said, gesturing to the Russian as she rose and slipped the sunglasses back over her eyes. "I have better things to do anyway."

She left without a backward glance and went to the laptop to listen to Stasia's act.

The Italian spy's accented Russian came through the speakers clearly. "Americans. They have no finesse," she said.

Olivia heard the crackle of a water bottle followed by a moment of what could only be gulping as the Russian drank.

A moment later, Stasia said, "She is probably preparing the car battery even as we speak."

Olivia admired how lightly Stasia delivered this threat.

"It will be a waste of time," said the Russian. He sucked in an audible breath. "You will learn nothing from me." He cleared his throat and spat. "She will break before I do."

Silence filled the room for a moment. Olivia wondered how her partner would respond.

"I would not be so sure about that," Stasia said at last, her voice strangely compelling. On the heels of that comment came the crackle of the water bottle before the Italian operative continued. "My American friend has worked on her all night to no avail. Your boss likely hired her because he knows that she is former Czech special forces."

After dropping this juicy tidbit—which Olivia suspected was true though Beta had never mentioned it—Stasia said no more.

A moment later, she sat next to Olivia at their table.

"That was some brilliant work," said Olivia, glancing at the other woman. "You interrogate as well as you shoot."

Stasia shrugged. "I would rather convince with words than wound with bullets. But we shall see if Ivan will be receptive to her approach."

"Can you handle this by yourself? It looks like it will take all day, and I need to make a phone call."

Stasia nodded. "Of course. Your asset?" When Olivia hesitated, she asked, "Or your fiancé?"

"Neither," said Olivia, reluctantly. "An old friend at the Agency. I'm troubled by Bryk's appearance last night."

"You are thinking that whoever supplied him with the latest generation of Czech weapons perhaps alerted him to an intrusion on his secure phone."

Olivia nodded. "My contact has access to the latest tech the Agency uses. He'll know what's possible, which may give us enough information to keep a repeat of last night from happening." She stood, slipping her sunglasses into her jacket pocket. "Text me if you need a hand."

Stasia nodded and turned her attention back to the audio streaming from the laptop.

Olivia walked outside into the desolate abandoned train yard where the early morning sun left deep shadows along the foundations of the empty buildings. The pungent scent of decomposing flesh mixed with the weedy decay, spiking a headache between her eyes. She ignored it and dialed the number of her old CIA mentor, Sam Ahren.

He picked up on the third ring. "I thought you were in Rome," he said without preamble.

"I had to help a friend with a dog," she said.

He didn't press her for details. Instead, he said, "You always did have a soft heart. Let me know if you need a vet reference."

Sam knew that Olivia had gone off the reservation, and he still had her back.

"Thanks, but that's not necessary. What you can do is tell me whether there's a cellphone that alerts the caller that it's been stung by a ray."

"There is one, sold by an American company. It's a standard cellphone running heavily modified operating software, including a baseband firewall that identifies fake cell attacks."

"How likely do you think it is that a Polish syndicate boss would have one?"

"I guess it's not impossible, but I doubt it. It just came on the market last week."

"Hm," said Olivia, thinking. Then she changed subjects. "Listen, I do have a favor to ask."

"Anything."

"Can you check around and see who's running my former Russian asset out of the Prague station? My Spidey sense is tingling. I want to make sure she's not being led astray."

"Will do." Sam paused before asking, "Are you sure you want out of the field, Olivia? Your instincts are as good as any I've ever seen in a field officer."

Étienne's dear face wavered in her memory. For a moment, Olivia's longing for him clogged her throat shut. She cleared it with effort. "It's good to talk to you, Sam. We should get a drink soon."

Sam didn't push. "Anytime. Just tell me where, and I'm there."

Olivia ended the call and returned inside where Stasia sat listening to the audio streaming from the hidden FM transmitters. Grunting and noise filled the laptop's speakers, attesting to a violent struggle inside the holding cell.

"You haven't gone in to break that up yet?" asked Olivia, starting toward the door. She'd let herself get distracted on an operation. A potentially fatal error.

Stasia didn't look as she reached out to grab Olivia's arm, halting her momentum. "She has not signaled for help." She glanced at Olivia and shrugged. "You would only disrupt her play by going in."

"And what play is that?" asked Olivia, incipient curiosity wrestling with her alarm.

Despite the urgency of the situation and Beta's nature, she hadn't expected Beta to challenge Bryk's Bratva lieutenant so soon. Perhaps the Russian criminal had attacked the weaker inmate in a bid to keep her quiet. ...

Stasia returned her attention to the audio. "The play where she tells Ivan that there is a mole in Bryk's organization and that Bryk sent her to kill him. That she knows that he has been talking to us. She insisted that we are even now dismantling Bryk's sex-trafficking operation with his help. Of course, he responded to that provocation."

Olivia stared at Stasia until the other operative looked at her. "How does that make sense given that he thinks we grabbed her first?"

Stasia lifted her chin toward the room as she answered Olivia's question. "It makes sense if we picked her up on that errand, *sì*? She told him that he is a dead man, but he asserts his loyalty. He will be desperate to prove that he is not compromised. You will see. I give her another fifteen seconds before he yields."

Desire to trust Stasia's assessment warred with Olivia's protective instincts. "Fifteen seconds and no more," she said.

Almost instantly, the violence they heard over the audio feed intensified. For a moment, Olivia's heart skipped an icy beat as she heard several loud thuds, panting, and a low feral scream from Beta that caused her hackles to rise. Olivia went for her handgun in its holster on her hip. Stasia came up from her seat as she leaned toward the laptop, her grip on the table's edge belying her restraint.

Then Beta hissed a warning to the Russian, who responded in a nearly unintelligible croak. "Wait! I can prove my loyalty. Take me with you. I will show you that the stock is safe. The Americans and Italians have no idea where they are."

"Then show me, polar dog, or I slit your throat here and now. I will not remain another minute while you give away the keys to Bryk's operation."

What the hell did that mean?

Olivia stood so fast her chair crashed to the floor. She lunged for the door of the interrogation room, throwing it wide as Stasia came to a halt behind her, the Benelli shotgun at her shoulder ready to use.

Only to see the Russian crawling through a jagged opening in the exterior wall that hadn't been there the day before, leaving behind an empty room.

EIGHT

"**C**rap!" said Olivia, pivoting and rushing past Stasia toward the entry door.

Stasia followed Olivia outside just in time for them to hear a motorcycle on the far side of the building rev its engine. They sprinted along the side of the building, their progress impeded by the tall weeds that pulled at their legs. As they reached the corner, Beta came roaring past with the Russian behind her on the seat.

Taking half a second to plant her feet, Olivia lifted her weapon and fired at the speeding motorcycle. Her shots just missed the rear tire as Beta skidded sideways to avoid them.

Stasia, who still carried the Nova, an Italian pump-action shot, refrained from shooting at the fast-receding vehicle and its riders, which had quickly gone beyond its range.

Instead, she said, "That is the second time that she has not followed the plan."

Olivia heard what the Italian operative left unsaid: *are you certain that the Czech is not playing both sides for her own purposes?*

Ignoring Stasia, she sprinted back into the main room and toward their makeshift work area. Beta had to have left some way to track the motorcycle. It was the only thing that made sense.

There! That small bag under Olivia's chair.

She dashed over, scooping it up. Inside she found a burner smartphone with a GPS tracking application enabled. The target being tracked headed to the northeast.

"Got them!" she said. "Beta has a tracker. She's going to lead us to the women and children."

She hoisted her large duffel bag which held extra ammunition clips and Semtex before grabbing her SRM M1208 semi-automatic shotgun. Yet when she turned to head out the door, she found Stasia leaning against the table with her own combat shotgun cradled in her arms and her crossed.

Olivia pulled up short.

"Waiting for something?" she asked, glancing at the Italian spy.

Stasia shrugged. "Convince me that Captain Czerná is not leading us into an ambush as she did last night. You spoke to your contact. Tell me that he confirmed that this Polish crime boss has technology capable of detecting an IMSI intrusion."

Frustration at the delay seized Olivia. Her St. Michael medal heated against her bare skin. She blew out a breath.

"He did not," she said.

Stasia tilted her head and studied her a moment. "Yet you still believe that Captain Czerná simply changes tactics in the field only when necessary?"

Now Olivia's frustration boiled over. "We don't have time to discuss this right now. She's point on this operation, for Godsake. You know as well as anyone what that means. She has to trust that we'll follow her lead when things change on the ground."

"You are not giving in to wishful thinking?" asked Stasia. Olivia almost felt the words probe her head and heart. "You are quite determined to rescue these innocents without having concrete evidence that they exist."

Olivia blinked, taken aback. Was she, in fact, blinded by her desire to rescue Bryk's victims? She gripped the medal between her fingers. Its heat seared them.

She swallowed and cleared her throat. "Beta and I have rescued others held by Bryk," she said, aware that time fled as they debated. "More importantly, there *is* a phone that detects fake cell towers. Figuring out how Bryk got it is for another day, however."

Stasia nodded and rose. "Then I will accept your faith in her."

Relief flooded Olivia. She nodded and tossed the burner phone to Stasia before striding to the rental car, the Italian spy now on her heels. They dropped their heavy gear bags into the backseat where they could access weapons and ammo as needed. Then Olivia took the driver's seat while Stasia, appropriately enough, took shotgun, her Benelli Nova resting in her lap.

Stasia navigated using the tracking app as a guide. It led them to the S86 expressway toward Sosnowiec, an industrial city about fifteen minutes' drive from Katowice.

The tracker led them to a large warehouse complex not far from where S86 crossed Route 94. A motorcycle sat in front of the smallest building with only three units at the back of the lot. Three loading docks with overhead doors gave access to the units.

Olivia drove to the north side of the windowless building where they could park unseen. By now, the June morning had turned sunny and warm, and the large expanse of concrete around the three buildings radiated heat as they stepped out of the car.

Olivia discarded the suit jacket she wore, instead putting on a tactical body-armor vest. Its weight reassured her as she clipped on a tactical knife and field medical kit and transferred ammo to its pouches. She pulled out her secondary weapon, a Glock 19, from its hip holster and checked the clip. While she did this, Stasia donned a bulletproof vest and checked her own sidearm. They both slipped Bluetooth headphones over their ears and double checked that they'd paired them with their cellphones. Not exactly a tactical headset but good enough.

Stasia looked at Olivia over the hood of the car. "Which unit do you think Bryk's man keeps them in?"

"The middle unit. That's where I'd stash them anyway."

"We cannot use Semtex to breach without risking the lives of everyone inside."

Olivia squinted at the two buildings perpendicular to the target warehouse. "It's too bad we can't get you onto the roof." She glanced toward the rear of the building. "Or had access to chains and a large truck...."

"Or we simply wait until Captain Czerná walks them out the door," said Stasia, tilting her head toward the front of the building.

Olivia listened. The sounds of voices drifted to her.

She caught Stasia's gaze. "Which approach do you want?"

"Mm," said Stasia, a mischievous light coming into her eyes. "I would like to surprise Ivan."

Olivia nodded, a small smile playing at the corners of her mouth. "Done. I'll hold his attention until you get in position."

Stasia swiveled and jogged behind the building.

Olivia crept to the corner of the warehouse and scouted around it. As she'd surmised, the activity came from the middle loading dock, where Beta and the unnamed Russian now stood. Before Olivia could step out and make herself known, the sounds of a vehicle caused them to turn around. On the far side of the lot, a large panel truck turned into the entrance.

She said a silent prayer of gratitude that she and Stasia had arrived when they had. It would be much better for the victims to be loaded into the truck before they made their move.

Olivia called Stasia. "See what I see?"

"*Sì.*"

"Be ready to move once they're on the truck."

"Copy that."

Olivia watched as a group of women and children and even a couple of teenage boys stumbled from the warehouse and across the loading ramp. From the bedraggled looks of their hair and crumpled clothing, it was clear that they had been confined in the spartan warehouse for days. Rage burned her gut when a little girl, jostled by the other victims, fell to the pavement. Beta swooped in and picked her up almost as soon as she touched the ground, but the girl never made a sound or moved.

Sixty seconds later, the Russian stepped up to lock the lift gate after all of the people in the warehouse had been forced inside.

That was Olivia's cue.

Swinging her M1208 to her shoulder, Olivia stepped around the corner of the warehouse as Bryk's man turned to face Beta. He reached for his Glock pistol, which he'd tucked into the back of his pants. Beta remained still.

The sound of a shotgun being pumped stopped his arm while it was still behind his back.

"Ah, ah, ah," said Stasia. She'd crept up on the Russian's blind spot and now stood within a couple of meters where she'd be able to take off his head with a single shot.

Olivia, her shotgun aimed at Beta, continued forward toward the truck. She and Bryk's man watched Olivia's approach with hard gazes.

"We'll take it from here," said Olivia.

While Stasia stood guard, Olivia disarmed both Beta and the Bratva handler, whose glare would have melted her if she'd cared. She didn't. He also kept up a stream of running abuse in Russian that she ignored as she bound him, except to tighten the flexi-cuffs until they cut into the skin of his wrists and ankles. Then she moved to cuff Beta.

Beta, who'd said nothing to this point, said, "Better kill me, American. Or I will become your worst nightmare."

"Yeah, yeah," said Olivia, not looking at the Czech. She tugged the flexi-cuffs closed, leaving a bit of wiggle room. "Give Bryk my best when you see him."

Then she and Stasia left the two tied together with the truck driver on the loading dock and drove away, Olivia behind the wheel of the truck while Stasia drove the rental car.

As they'd planned, Olivia drove the victims half an hour west to Gliwice where volunteers from New Hope, the British NGO that she'd worked with previously, would take charge of them. Kira arrived while Olivia helped with basic medical assessment of the twenty-three women, teens, and children. She'd found the little girl who'd fallen first and diagnosed a concussion—something she might have died from if left in the Russian's tender care.

Then Olivia drove the truck to the warehouse where Bryk's arms shipments had been stored and set it on fire.

For her part, Stasia returned to the locomotive depot and removed all evidence of their interrogation before returning to Rome. She left the intelligence that they'd gathered on Bryk at the Café Savoy and a voicemail to Olivia about the drop.

Once she'd returned to Bryk, Beta accused the Bratva lieutenant of being a mole for the SVR, Russian foreign intelligence.

Her evidence? His use of Sistema, a Russian martial art, which he'd betrayed in their encounter, and the polar-wolf tattoo. No one sentenced to a maximum-security prison in Russia left while a young man, if at all. Certainly not an unbroken one.

And he'd been out of touch for more than an hour after they'd surprised him meeting with the American and Italian. She left it to Bryk to fit all of the pieces together.

"Unfortunately for him," she said to Olivia later when they met at a hotel next to the Katowice International Airport, "he really is an SVR officer. Bryk has a source who confirmed that he is Major Alexei Volkov. I do not think Major Volkov will return to Moscow with honors."

"That's worrying in and of itself," said Olivia.

Beta nodded. "Agreed."

Olivia, who shuffled through the pile of documents that Stasia had recovered for her, stopped when she reached the large brown-paper envelope. She looked at Beta.

"Do you recognize this intel?" asked Olivia, sliding the documents across the table in the hotel bar.

Beta narrowed her eyes as she accepted the packet. She looked up sharply at the photos of Bryk. "Where did you get these?"

"I found them among the other intel at the train depot after we returned with Major Volkov. I thought they came from Andrej and Eliska, but I just realized that the dates on the call log stretch back almost a year."

Beta studied the log for several long moments before going through the photos.

"I recognize this place," she said after she'd looked at each one. "It is the Ostrava Airport."

"It looks like some sort of military exhibition."

"It is what my country calls 'NATO Days,' which is free to the public to show our defense and security capabilities. Czech armed forces display military equipment and weapons. Armed forces from various countries demonstrate their training, including units from the U.S."

"And arms manufacturers also participate?" asked Olivia, staring at a photo of Bryk talking to two men in suits standing behind a table. A partially visible corporate banner hung on the wall in the rear.

"Yes. It is an opportunity for Czech companies to sell to the militaries of other countries."

Olivia looked up and held Beta's gaze. "Could Bryk have purchased the Skorpions directly from the manufacturer?"

"Perhaps, but I think it unlikely. The company that makes the Skorpions would not want to risk its contract with my government." Beta gathered all of the intel and slipped it back into the envelope.

"Stasia Fiore must have supplied this intel, though why AISE would have surveillance on Bryk is curious."

Olivia shook her head. "She was there when I found it and said nothing. But she has been trying to track a Predator drone that was stolen from the Italian Air Force and sold by a Serbian arms dealer last summer, so perhaps someone from AISE made it to NATO days last fall."

"Hm," said Beta, appearing to consider this. "Regardless of its provenance, I would like to take this to Andrej and Eliska. It could lead us to Bryk's supplier."

Nodding, Olivia said, "Keep me in the loop. There's something really odd going on here."

Beta tilted her head. "Do you mean the distinct influence of an intelligence player?"

"Yeah," said Olivia. "Like the pull of a black hole."

"Either way, it is time to move on Bryk. He is not stupid and will soon start to pull at the loose threads of my story. Besides, I am tired of deferring to the mission. I look forward to interrogating him about his connections." The way she said this sent chills down Olivia's spine.

But it was time for her to return to her own agency. As Olivia started to take her leave, Beta stopped her.

"There is another odd thing, Olivia." The Czech officer paused, looking decidedly uncomfortable, which said something in and of itself. "At Club Pomarańcza ... the giant male and the blonde?"

Olivia nodded, remembering the civilians who'd appeared in the midst of their gunfight.

Beta seemed reluctant to continue. It set Olivia's antennae buzzing. She waited with bated breath despite herself.

Beta turned away, pacing around the hotel room. "I–I saw them take out two of Bryk's men who had line of sight on you. At the same time, Bryk's gun malfunctioned."

When she stopped and looked at Olivia, her haunted gaze called forth a strange vibrating in Olivia's medal. "Bryk's men had third-degree burns on their hands. *He* will never hold a gun in the same hand again."

Olivia thought about Beta's words all during the flight back to Rome as she toyed with the medal her college karate *sensei* had given her. There might be an unknown intelligence player in the Czech's operation, but there seemed to be something much harder to define in her own intelligence career.

When she returned to the Rome station the next day, she learned that Merjam and Esad had been transferred stateside. Olivia sucked in a deep breath and prayed that Merjam would be treated gently before she closed herself into an empty office to call Sam. She'd be heading out to France tomorrow, but she wanted to know that Marina too was safe.

"Markham," said Sam when he answered. "I was just about to call you."

Something in his voice warned Olivia.

"What is it?"

"There's no record at the Prague station of your former asset being run by anyone."

"Are you sure?" asked Olivia.

"Absolutely. It's possible she's being handled in a less formal manner, through discretionary funds. Your old boss, Reardon, has a reputation for doing that."

"Yeah, he had this pavement artist he paid off the books to keep him up-to-date on the local criminal element. He used him to follow me last year."

Olivia recalled the sly, yet confident, tone in Marina's voice when she'd told Olivia about her new espionage role.

Suddenly, she knew that's what had happened. "It's Reardon," she said before Sam could speak. "He's running her."

"Sounds like you don't think that's a good thing."

"My gut says it's not."

"Well, I trust your gut. Plus, I don't like Reardon. He's a little weasel of a bureaucrat who resents officers who live by their wits in the field. I can take a little more time and talk to Marina, figure out what scheme he's got cooking."

Relief washed through Olivia. "Thanks. That means a lot. Hey, I've got a question for you. Do you think Julia would like a little off-the-books financial mystery to solve?"

"Knowing Julia, she's bored out of her mind right now on that Russian-doll-like case she's working. Does this have something to do with your little side gig?"

"Yeah. Someone with intelligence links has been helping this vile Polish crime boss buy the latest shiny Czech weaponry."

"This the guy who sold the nuclear detonator package to a Kosovar terrorist last year?"

"Yeah."

"Anything I can do to help take scum like him out of business, I'll do. But you'd better be careful. It could be the Russians helping your Polish businessman."

"I don't think so. We just outed an SVR mole in his operation."

"Ah. This sounds serious. How do you get yourself into these predicaments?" Olivia heard humor and affection in his voice.

"I don't know, Sam. I just follow my conscience."

"Don't ever change, Markham. Don't ever change." He paused. "Looks like we won't get to have that drink for a while, but when we do, I have something I want to give you."

Olivia, playing with her engagement ring, said, "I'll be in France tomorrow. You know where to find me."

Olivia spent the rest of the morning finalizing paperwork related to her transfer to the Paris office and her final, impromptu mission as the Kotor housekeeper. She studied the final action report that the Agency's recovery expert, Miles Baxter, had written for context for her own report. Every time she read about Imam Alami and a trio of his followers invading the hospital where they killed Baxter's injured teammate and the surgical team who'd been desperately trying to save his life, fury scalded her. Baxter had taken down the trio in a gunfight that wounded him, but Imam Alami, true to his cockroach nature, had scuttled away.

She was rereading Esad's interrogation transcript when Julia returned her earlier voicemail.

"Hey, Ju-Ju!" she said with affection.

It had been more than a year-and-a-half since she'd last seen her former teammate, and that hadn't been under the best circumstances. Their reunion had been at the funeral for another teammate, Monica, who'd died in a terrorist bombing.

"Liv. It's good to hear your voice. Reminds me of a time before the glowing blue screen captured my soul," said Julia. Despite her words, she sounded cheerful. "Sam says you've got something that needs my forensic accounting expertise."

"Strictly a favor, Julia," said Olivia, her gaze snagging on something in the interrogation report in front of her. She began rifling through the rest of the documents in the case file as she continued. "Can you do a deep dive on the Prague station's finances, including the station chief, Henry Reardon?"

It was the kind of favor that Olivia had often called upon Julia to provide after their first mission together, when she was put on a team to root out corruption in the SAD division.

"Sure. Anything in particular I should be looking for?"

"Connections to Czech weapons manufacturers, NATO, arms deals, official trips to Poland. I don't want to limit you. Just see if anything odd emerges."

"Will do."

Olivia paused at the picture of a Venetian marina where Esad had met Alami and his cell last June. "How big is a Predator drone?"

"Let me check." There was a pause while Julia did a quick Internet search. "A little more than eight meters long, but twice that in wingspan. Why?"

"I think I just found where one stolen by terrorists has been stored for the past year."

Right under AISE's nose the whole time.

NINE

As it happened, Olivia's return to France got delayed another twelve hours. When she'd called Stasia with her suspicion that Imam Alami had stored the stolen Predator drone in a boathouse in Venice, the Italian operative had immediately invited her to join her team when they raided the site.

"But you don't even know if I'm right," said Olivia, laughing.

"*Bella*, I do not need to wait for confirmation to invite you or call a team together. Your theory fits the pieces of our puzzle together. Please tell me that the handsome French doctor can wait a few more hours. I will personally escort you to Paris on a private flight courtesy of my government. It is the least I can do."

Olivia's hunch proved true. Motivated AISE analysts ran down more than a years' worth of marina records while a small team of field officers compiled surprisingly thorough surveillance on the marina in a matter of hours.

Excitement and disappointment warred within Olivia. She hated telling Étienne yet again that she wouldn't be reuniting with him as planned but seeing with her own eyes that the Italians had recovered the Predator more than justified the delay.

Even before the surveillance had been fully analyzed, Stasia sent a car for Olivia. After a short drive, they boarded a helicopter which flew them to a private airfield outside Venice where they met the same commando team that had raided the palazzo a year before. Major Antonelli, the granite-eyed special-forces commander, simply nodded at Olivia as she took her place next to Stasia during the mission briefing.

Alami had left watchers, two young men whom Italian intelligence confirmed had immigrated from North Africa the previous year. One had been employed by the marina, which made his guard job less obvious and his post more constrained, but the other watcher had been observed in various public areas. Olivia suspected that there was a whole team of floaters who rotated through guard duty. The Italians would have their hands full trying to round them all up.

As the point on the mission, Stasia approached the boathouse, peering inside as if looking for someone, but in actuality confirming that the drone—or at least something its size and shape—occupied the building. Within minutes, the marina employee moved to intercept her. He alerted the floating guard, who stood up from his table on the patio outside a trendy restaurant and began to walk toward the boathouse. Olivia left her position at a nearby table to follow him.

Five minutes later, both men had been restrained and cuffed while Major Antonelli's men descended on the formerly tranquil marina scene, transforming it into controlled chaos.

Olivia, who stood next to Stasia with her arms crossed, watched as the commandos removed the tarp concealing the stolen Predator drone inside the boathouse.

"Are you going to miss this, *cara*?" asked Stasia, studying Olivia. "The excitement? The satisfaction at outwitting and out-maneuvering dangerous people?"

"Kicking butt and taking names?" asked Olivia. She looked at her friend. "Maybe a little."

"Have you heard anything about the special package we retrieved in Poland?"

"It arrived at its destination without incident."

"And the girl?" Stasia's voice sounded husky, and her gaze had grown intent.

"Has been seen by a doctor, had an MRI, and admitted to the hospital. She had a brain bleed, so they operated." At Stasia's widened eyes, Olivia laid her hand on her friend's forearm. "Her prognosis is good, Staz."

Stasia shook her head. "But she would not have been hurt if we had not pushed the Russian."

Olivia just looked at her, tilting her head slightly in an unspoken *oh, really?*

Stasia blinked and shifted.

Olivia moved on. "Did I tell you that the Russian was an SVR officer named Ivan Volkov?"

Stasia's eyes widened again. "No!" She started laughing.

Olivia grinned.

Stasia grew serious. "What do you think your imam will do when he discovers that his Predator has been recovered?"

Olivia shrugged. "Who knows? Not my problem. I'm going to be living quietly in France. Speaking of which, how about that plane ride?"

Stasia's smile returned. "I think that Major Antonelli can oversee the final cleanup here. We can be wheels up in half an hour. Can your beloved wait a little longer?"

True to her word, Stasia had Olivia airborne within thirty minutes, though she didn't escort Olivia on the hour-and-a-half flight to Paris. It was late when Olivia finally made her way to the apartment that Étienne had rented on the left bank of the Seine in the 13th *arrondissement*, or district, between the hipster Latin Quarter in the north and the vibrant Quartier Asiatique in the southeast. Not far from the Necker hospital where he held his primary job, the working-class neighborhood was convenient to half a dozen other hospitals, including the public Hôpital D'enfants across the river in the 12th district.

Olivia picked the ancient lock on the front door of the small apartment building sited on a narrow unlit cobblestone lane off Rue de la Butte aux Cailles before repeating the maneuver on the apartment's front door. She left her roll-on suitcase and shoes just inside the door, waiting while her eyes adjusted to the darkness. She didn't recognize any of the furniture and wondered if Étienne had rented the apartment fully furnished. She did, however, recognize Cleo, who padded on silent paws toward her, demanding attention until she picked him up.

After snuggling the disgruntled feline for a few blissful moments, she walked down the short hallway to the bedroom, stripping her clothes on her way, before slipping into bed next to the man that she loved.

If Olivia had had her way, they would have stayed in that bed for the next three days, living on love and stale croissants, but Étienne had an early shift at the hospital. Thinking about how little sleep he'd gotten the night before, Olivia smiled in gratitude that he didn't have any surgeries scheduled and rolled over to snuggle his pillow. For the first time since she'd left Kotor, Olivia slept soundly and woke feeling refreshed and relaxed.

It didn't last beyond her first cup of French-pressed coffee.

At 10:20, as Olivia sat in one of Étienne's shirts on the worn beige sofa flipping through a French oncology journal with one hand and holding a coffee cup in the other, Sam called.

"Hey, Sam," she said, shifting her focus from the cutting-edge nano delivery of cancer drugs to the world of espionage, "I hoped I'd hear from you by now. Have you talked to Marina?"

"I spoke to her briefly on the phone a couple of days ago, right after we got off the phone. We set a meeting for this morning at a coffee shop in Prague. But she never showed."

A warning zing raced through Olivia. She fingered her St. Michael medal in reaction.

"That's not like her," she said, sitting up and setting the journal and coffee cup down. "Did she tell you anything on the phone?"

"Not much. She just seemed spooked, said an SVR officer named Volkov disappeared a few days ago. She had some information on him and what he was doing. He wouldn't happen to be the same mole you outed, would he?"

The zing settled into a pool of cold acid in the pit of Olivia's stomach. "I ran into him on my side gig," she said. "He was living a legend as a Bratva lieutenant working for a Pole named Kacper Bryk. As part of our play, we needed a mole. It was sheer coincidence that we got it right. Bryk likely killed him."

"Something is starting to stink in the state of Denmark." Sam's metaphor would have been funny if it wasn't so ominous.

It also reminded her of something she'd failed to tell Sam earlier that now seemed very relevant.

"Marina mentioned a friend of Bryk's, an arms dealer named Bogdi Król. He negotiated a sale of a nuclear detonator last year that we derailed. She said she had information on Król that the CIA would be interested in."

"He the one that Popov approached first?"

"Yes."

Sam swore. "I misspoke. This isn't starting to stink. It reeks to high heaven. And *my* Spidey sense says it has something to do with your old friend Reardon."

Olivia sighed and pinched the bridge of her nose. "I think I suspected this all along," she said. "I asked Julia to look into the Prague station's finances."

"I'd better stay in Prague a little longer, do some more poking around. I hope your friend has decided to take a little vacation because I don't like the alternatives."

"Me either," said Olivia. "Stay safe, Sam."

"My head's on a swivel," he said before hanging up.

Abandoning her plans to stay in Étienne's shirt the whole day, Olivia got dressed and spent the afternoon calling various contacts she'd made in Europe who could help her gather weapons and ammunition for a rainy-day cache. She also reviewed her bugout bag, which she'd brought with her to Paris out of habit. She hadn't actually thought she'd ever need it again, but then she hadn't expected the Kotor safehouse to be attacked or seasoned CIA operatives killed.

Her afternoon preparations did wonders for her nerves. By the time Étienne returned home from the hospital, she had a traditional vegetable tian in the oven and a bottle of Cabernet Sauvignon open to breathe.

Étienne collapsed on the sofa next to her with an audible sigh. Olivia handed him a full wineglass.

He picked up one of her hands with his free hand, toying with her fingers before threading his own long, elegant ones through them. Olivia had fallen in love with his hands first. They'd been so gentle, yet so sure, with the silent, wide-eyed Nika. She'd had a strong yearning for him that she now recognized as the desire to see him hold their child in those hands.

Étienne looked at her. "Are you trying to distract me from the conversation that we need to have about who you really are?" His voice, when he spoke, was even, but Olivia heard the edge it held.

"No." Olivia shook her head. "Just hoping to show you a little how sorry I am that I didn't tell you the truth before, *mon amour*. And also hoping that it will be harder for you to stay angry at me if your stomach is full."

"I am not angry, Olivia, just bewildered and hurt." Étienne turned the wineglass in his hand and then took a sip. "The truth is, I wonder how I can trust that you love me." He said this without looking at her.

Olivia reached for the wineglass and, taking it from him, set it on the coffee table. She slipped onto her knees and reached for his face, placing both palms on either side of it as she turned his reluctant gaze to meet hers.

"And that's why I love you and wish you were angry with me. You *should* be angry with me. The truth is that I should never have started a relationship with you in which I couldn't be completely honest. But I followed my heart." Olivia stopped there, holding Étienne's gaze so that he could see all of the love, regret, and worry roiling inside of her.

Étienne's dark eyes studied her for an agonizing moment, and then he leaned forward and kissed her, long and slow and filled with promise. When he sat back, he asked, "When will we eat? That smells delicious, and it has been hours since I managed to eat a teria baguette and brie."

A day later, Olivia hadn't heard anything from Sam about Marina or from Julia about Reardon. When she called Sam's cellphone, he didn't pick up, and the voice mailbox was full. That was a signal that he'd abandoned the phone. She then left a message on a dating Web site where they'd set up accounts years before for emergency contact, but he hadn't responded within four hours—not necessarily a bad sign, but definitely not a good one.

Julia, on the other hand, answered with an apology. "Sorry, Liv. I haven't had time to dig into the Prague station. We just got slammed with a whole new snakes' nest of financials on this private-security contractor masquerading as a telecommunications company. I did run a basic reconciliation on station accounts, and they don't match projections, but that might just be a temporary discrepancy. You know that in the real world cash doesn't flow as evenly and predictably as accountants' budgets."

Olivia, disappointed and starting to feel a pinch in the spot on her upper back that made an ideal target for a distant, unseen shooter, took the metro towards one of the Agency's many safehouses in Paris. At least for the time being, she was being slotted into an existing site without a NOC, but that would change in the coming weeks when the CIA opened up a new HANDS Across Borders clinic, either in the 18th arrondissement or Saint-Denis, just north of it over the Seine. Given her experience and background, she'd bet on Saint-Denis with the largest Magrebhi population in the Paris area.

As she boarded the subway, the pinch bloomed across her back and up her neck. Olivia took a position next to one of the doors and carefully studied the occupants reflected in the windows. Whoever surveilled her was good. She had no idea which of the people, reading cellphones and books, sleeping or staring at the floor or at nothing, followed her.

Nevertheless, she initiated an SDR, a surveillance detection route, which took her on an extended tour of Paris and its top tourist attractions. She even stopped to have a *café au lait* in a sidewalk café and to call the housekeeper on duty at her new post to explain the situation. He sounded skeptical but given that they couldn't afford for the site to be compromised, he told her brusquely to feel free to show up to work as soon as she'd lost her tail.

She never identified her watchers.

It had to be multiple people working in a zone, tag-team protocol. That in itself was troubling. It suggested a level of sophistication employed by state-level intelligence operations, who could afford to field a skilled and large team.

Against her.

Something told Olivia it *wasn't* an official intelligence operation, though. Nothing that she'd had her fingers in during the past year had been sanctioned by any government, not even the Russian general selling a nuclear detonator on the side.

Strangely, her nerves settled after a few hours. Whoever it was only watched. There didn't seem to be any intent for something more aggressive, like a snatch-and-grab. Or assassination.

At least not yet.

Olivia shuddered at the thought and tapped her St. Michael medal. Calm returned.

She left the café and wandered some more, sticking to public, crowded places and browsing through small shops. Eventually fury began to build inside her. She couldn't live like this indefinitely. It was better for her and for the Agency if she turned the tables on the entity running surveillance on her. Besides, she couldn't go back to the apartment. And neither could Étienne.

She absolutely hated to tell him that her secret life had intruded again, this time threatening their home. But when she called the hospital to warn him to stay away from the apartment, he didn't answer. She looked at her watch. It was only 3 p.m. His shift wouldn't end for another hour. He was probably meeting with a patient or even at a departmental meeting. Nevertheless, unease pricked Olivia. She pulled up short.

If they'd found her in Paris, they'd also found Étienne. ...

Sudden panic gripped Olivia, and she abandoned all pretense at sightseeing and flagged down a taxi. When she arrived at the Necker, she raced to the oncology department where no one had seen Étienne since lunch. They even paged him to no avail.

Olivia's heart raced. It made no sense that none of the staff could explain where Étienne was. Then again, it made no sense that anyone would be capable of snatching a doctor in a busy hospital with security on every floor without someone seeing something. He must be in the building somewhere. ...

Calling Étienne's phone again, Olivia darted toward the elevator, intending to head to the security office to demand to view the hospital's security videos from the afternoon. Just as Olivia reached the open door, a woman hurrying down the corridor called out to her.

"Excusez-moi, mademoiselle!"

Olivia, who'd failed to scan the environment despite her training, raised her gaze to take in the other woman. She appeared to be in her early thirties with dark hair and shadowed eyes. Her rumpled clothes suggested that she'd slept in them.

"*Oui?*" asked Olivia as the elevator door closed behind her. She guessed that a mother of one of the pediatric patients addressed her.

"Please forgive me. I overheard you asking about Dr. Dumond. He is my son's doctor. He was with Luc when the Hôpital Cochin called and asked him to come for an emergency consult."

Olivia took a deep breath, forcing her heartrate to slow. She'd forgotten that Étienne had arrangements with other Paris hospitals.

"What time was this?" she asked as she ended the unanswered call.

"Around one-thirty p.m."

"*Merci,*" said Olivia, pivoting to head back to the nurses' station.

The other woman touched her forearm. "I hope that nothing is wrong, *mademoiselle*. Dr. Dumond is my son's best hope."

Olivia blinked. Then she mentally shook herself and laughed a little, waving her hand. "I only arrived in Paris two days ago. I'm not yet used to my fiancé's busy schedule."

The mother nodded, and Olivia continued to the nurses' station where a harried-looking woman in nurses' scrubs reviewed a chart. Olivia had spoken to her only minutes before. When she looked up at Olivia's approach, annoyance flitted across her face.

Olivia ignored it. "Would you have a record of a request for a consult for Dr. Dumond from the Hôpital Cochin?"

"I would, but I do not."

Olivia persisted despite her heart now hammering against her ribcage. The St. Michael medal burned her chest through her blouse. "But could he have gotten a direct call and left without telling you?"

The woman stopped flipping pages in the folder and slammed the cover shut. "*Oui*, but I hope that Dr. Dumond respects the Necker staff enough to extend the courtesy of letting us know that he would be leaving us short-staffed this afternoon." Her pointed tone said that Olivia clearly didn't understand the requirements of courtesy.

Olivia was about to insist that the nurse call the Hôpital Cochin when her cellphone rang.

Étienne.

She turned from the cranky nurse as she answered.

"Étienne, thank God! I was beginning to worry!" Olivia's breathless voice gave the lie to her attempt at a casual tone.

Behind her, she sensed the nurse listening. She paced away from the desk.

"I am sorry to have alarmed you, *ma cherie*. It could not be helped, I am afraid," said Étienne in a strained voice.

"What is it? What's happened?" asked Olivia sprinting now to the stairs. She had to get out of this veritable prison of a hospital.

"Please do not wait for me for dinner this evening." There was an odd noise followed by a painful pause before Étienne continued, his words halting. "Your old friend Imam Alami sends his regrets, but he will be hosting me for the foreseeable future."

"Put him on the phone," said Olivia as she slammed the door to the stairs open.

The line went dead.

Then Olivia's cellphone chimed with a notification.

When she looked at the image that had been texted from Étienne's phone, she saw her beloved, his face battered and bruised.

Below it the text simply said, "Wait for instructions."

TEN

For the first time since her cousin Emily had been murdered the summer before she started college, Olivia knew despair. This time, it was different. At 18, she couldn't know what was coming. Now, she had every understanding of what the future held.

Alami had Étienne. He was dead unless she could manage a miracle. And she had no reason to believe that she could by herself.

Then everything went from horrible to impossible.

Beta called as Olivia wended her way through the Sèvres-Lecourbe metro station. "Bryk has been released."

That derailed Olivia's focus for only a moment. "Sorry to hear that, but I'm afraid I can't help this time, Beta. I've got my own problem to deal with."

Olivia boarded a packed train, ensuring that her watcher followed before she slipped off at the last moment.

"It gets worse," said Beta as Olivia raced towards the stairs. "An American intelligence officer picked him up. He said he was running Bryk." She paused. "He identified you as Bryk's weapons supplier."

Despite her distraction, Olivia laughed in disbelief. "Yeah, right. I managed a lot of gun deals from Montenegro. Wait," she said as a thought hit her, "this play only works if I had help. You?"

"Yes." Beta's terse answer held a world of meaning. "Andrej tipped me off."

"So, you're on the run, too."

Beta's lack of answer was answer enough. Instead, she asked, "What happened, Liv?" Her voice had sharpened, if possible.

Olivia turned back before the exit to the street and went down the stairs again. The train had exited the station with her watcher. She felt no other eyes on her at the moment.

"Not much. Just an old friend looked me up in Paris."

"Anyone that I know?"

"Unless you know murderous Magrebhi *jihadis*, I don't think so."

As she answered, Olivia boarded another metro train heading in the same direction as the first. Whatever training Alami's team had, they wouldn't expect her to do that. Still, she'd feel more secure once she was certain that she'd lost her tail.

And had more firepower than her Glock.

"Why do I suspect that you are not telling me everything?"

Beta's question surprised Olivia. She sighed and pinched the bridge of her nose. It wasn't really the time or place, but a lunch to confide in girlfriends had never been on her career plan.

"I was on my way out of the field, Beta. I spent the last year managing a safehouse in Kotor. I met someone there. Étienne." Olivia swallowed around a lump. "We're engaged to be married."

"You and Étienne are running from this murderous Magrebhi?"

"Imam Alami. He took Étienne." Olivia's voice broke. Beta waited while she composed herself. "I'm being surveilled by Alami's team. I shook them off, but it doesn't matter. Once Alami contacts me with instructions, I'll have no choice but to do whatever he says on the chance that I can save Étienne."

"That means that I can reach you via this number," said Beta.

"Yes."

"Good. I will contact you when I am able." Then Beta severed the connection.

The train eased to a stop at the Alexandre Dumas station. Olivia looked around. Several people were exiting, including a with a stroller, a small child, and a heavy bag filled with fresh vegetables.

Olivia stepped forward. *"S'il vous plait,"* she said, gesturing toward the canvas tote, "let me help with your bag."

The harried slid a critical look over Olivia just as the infant started to cry and the subway door to slide shut. She nodded.

The first that Olivia realized that she had more than Alami's guys following her happened shortly after she stepped off the train carrying the mother's bag. As she scanned the crowded platform, Olivia's gaze moved over a woman standing next to a vending machine and holding a phone to her ear. Although her head never shifted, the nondescript woman scanned Olivia as she walked past. It wasn't much, but the hairs on Olivia's neck shivered.

She needed to get to her weapons cache and go-bag. And she couldn't ditch this phone. Not yet anyway.

Olivia felt the woman fall in behind her and the oblivious mother. Her mind raced. How much time could she buy if she lured the other operative into an ambush somewhere?

If nothing else, she'd confirm that the CIA now tracked her.

Bitterness briefly burned Olivia's throat. Apparently, it didn't take long for one accusation to overshadow everything she'd accomplished in the Agency.

Her phone pinged with a text notification. *La Meridionale, Thursday, 20:00. Ticket at office in the name Amina El Filali.*

It was followed with another text. *Dr. Dumond cannot wait a week for the next ferry.*

Olivia helped the mother carry the stroller up the flight of stairs to street level where the woman boarded the 76 bus with her children and vegetables. As Olivia watched them, inspiration struck her.

She headed southeast, keeping a brisk pace so that the CIA operative was forced to drop back or risk exposure. For now, Olivia opted to remain in the open as if unaware of her tail and dialed the safehouse to which she'd been assigned. Perhaps something would shake out during the call. Either way, she'd reinforce the idea that she had no idea that the CIA followed her.

The housekeeper picked up after the third ring. "Reservations."

"Taylor Temp Services, Markham speaking."

"Markham, hey. Still being followed?" The housekeeper's voice had a much sweeter sound than it had earlier in the morning when Olivia first called. It was also insincere. This guy would have to improve if he ever hoped to survive in the field.

"Nope," she said, matching his tone. She'd made it to the intersection. As she turned right onto Avenue Philippe Auguste, she continued. "I ditched whoever it was in the La Chapelle station."

"That's good news. You get a gander at your tail?" The housekeeper said this so casually Olivia knew that he'd been read in on the Agency surveillance of her.

"Afraid not," she said to the housekeeper's subtle probing. "I'm going to take my time coming to you just in case."

Olivia glimpsed the female operative behind her in the reflective surface of a furniture store's windows. The woman had discarded her gray jacket and now wore a floppy hat, but Olivia recognized her profile and stature regardless.

"That's not a good idea, Markham. I need you here." He paused before adding, "So you got off the metro at La Chapelle?"

As if you don't know exactly where I am thought Olivia, but she said, "No. I left at Alexandre Dumas. I'm heading to Printemps now for a change of attire."

"Copy that," he said. "I'll get someone there in twenty minutes."

Genius certainly hadn't offered to help her out earlier when she said she had a skilled team of unknown operatives following her.

Olivia reached Cours de Vincennes where the iconic French department store had a location before she responded to the CIA officer. "Negative, Reservations. The city makes my neck itch. I'll contact you for pickup in one hour."

She hung up before he could protest. But it didn't matter. Her CIA tail would stay on her. Olivia needed to continue her ploy a little longer to lure the other operative into a place of her choosing, all the while picking up what she needed to travel to Marseille.

The CIA shadow faded away as Olivia turned left at the corner of the wide, busy boulevard. Olivia wasn't fooled. As long as she had her cellphone, the other field officer could wait in the vicinity and not fear losing her.

Olivia entered the department store and made her way to the women's clothing department where she chose an ankle-length dress in a plain, earthen color, two pairs of chino pants, one khaki gray and the other olive drab, a long-sleeved white shirt, a bra, and several pairs of underwear and socks. She then went to the accessories section where she found designer sunglasses with enormous lenses, three scarves of various colors and patterns, a backpack and handbag, and a rolling hardshell suitcase. Finally, she bought a sturdy pair of black-leather calf-high boots.

Olivia donned the sunglasses and tied one of the scarves in her hair before slipping the handbag over her shoulder. Everything else she stuffed into the suitcase, including her old crossbody bag. It wasn't much of a disguise, and the other CIA operative would expect her to change her appearance, but it would suffice to convince the woman that Olivia still didn't know that the CIA tracked her.

She exited Printemps and headed east on Cors de Vincennes, pulling the luggage next to her.

Three minutes later she entered the Vincennes metro station and boarded the subway headed to the Paris suburbs and Disneyland.

The Agency officer tailing her made it onto the train two cars behind Olivia's. Olivia waited until the train had nearly reached the next station before exchanging her scarf for a different one, this time tying it into a bandana-style at the side of her neck. Again, not much of a disguise, but enough of a change to delay the other operative's quick visual identification.

Although full, the train had far fewer passengers than it would in the next forty-five minutes as visitors to the Magic Kingdom left the park to return to Paris where commuters would cram the train after their workday in the city.

Olivia managed to sit down for the remainder of the thirty-minute trip to the American theme park. Fatigue washed over her, and she closed her eyes, letting her head fall back onto the window. Chattering voices soothed her for a moment, but then alert shrieked through her from head to toe. She let her eyelids rise a fraction so that she could scan nearby passengers.

That's when she saw him: the Company's master at bringing in the most challenging targets, Miles Baxter. He'd entered the train car at the far end and studied a blond woman sitting by herself diagonally from Olivia. Something in his expression suggested that he considered this woman a target.

Olivia, leaning forward as she pretended to search inside her purse, studied the blonde. The stranger had a similar build and hair color to her own. She even had the same hairstyle and wore similar clothing, including a headscarf. And she also pulled a wheeled suitcase.

When the train pulled into the final station, Marne-la-Vallée Chessy, the unknown blonde rose to sidle through the passengers lining in front of the sliding doors next to her seat. Baxter followed her, his intent gaze never straying from his target.

Olivia waited until she saw the female CIA officer crossing the platform through the train window. Then she too stood and exited the car, now behind the operatives assigned to follow her. For the moment at least, they'd lost a positive visual identification of her and wouldn't realize their mistake until and unless the gap between her and the doppelganger widened.

Olivia had no intention of letting that happen.

Still, what were the odds that her twin would appear just as she faced one of the best field operatives in the Agency?

It felt slightly miraculous.

Olivia's fingers went of their own accord to her St. Michael medal. It sure felt like someone looked out for her.

She shook her head to clear it. She had to dump her cellphone as soon as possible. Étienne's life depended on her evading CIA surveillance. It was unthinkable that the Company would listen to her now and stage a rescue of a lone French doctor who may or may not be held by a known terrorist.

Olivia's heaven-sent decoy led the trio of spooks towards Disneyland. When it became clear where this providential stand-in headed, Olivia threw her Glock into the nearest trash bin, tucking it among the refuse to hide it from a casual glance.

Yet another reason to get to her weapons cache. She wished she'd had time to stockpile more around Paris, even France. She didn't have nearly enough cash or connections to add to it.

The target entered the theme park alone before stopping at Guest Services to rent locker storage for her suitcase. Olivia risked exposure to leave her own luggage.

Then the target continued past the Main Street train station and the horse-drawn streetcars. Baxter and his teammate shadowed her while Olivia shadowed them, moving with relative ease among the crowd filled with families with small children and groups of young adults.

It was always easier to be the predator than the prey.

As for Olivia's twin, she surprised Olivia at how well she navigated the route, always managing to remain twenty meters in front of the female CIA officer.

Almost as if she'd been trained.

Olivia had no explanation for this, nothing plausible anyway.

Their unknown target walked through the Discovery Arcade on the northeast side of Main Street, causing Baxter to continue on the quaint avenue where Olivia knew that he'd take up position outside while the female CIA officer pretended to shop in a Christmas store across from the arcade. Olivia entered a boutique on the other side of Main Street.

Olivia pulled out her cellphone and sent a cryptic text to Beta. By now her employer had gotten into her phone. By now Beta's employer had gotten into *hers*. Olivia hoped that her friend would get this final text, but neither of them had anticipated that they'd be simultaneously out in the cold. Not that having a protocol for contacting Sam Ahren had kept *that* communication channel open. And, anyway, Stasia had gotten it right: relationships outside the job were impossible, and relationships inside were at best unreliable, at worst toxic.

A moment after Olivia hit *send*, the mysterious blonde who'd caught the CIA's attention wandered out of the arcade and headed toward Main Street. The female CIA officer followed thirty seconds later. As the blonde turned the corner onto the quintessential Disney thoroughfare where even now a boisterous parade of characters and musicians made its way from the roundabout behind them, she looked in Olivia's direction.

For an electric instant, Olivia thought that the stranger's gaze connected with hers, *really* connected. Bright blue eyes blazed in the late afternoon sun, sending a jolt down Olivia's spine. And then the woman turned back toward Main Street as she wended her way through the crowd gathered along the sidewalk to watch the parade.

Olivia blinked as if coming awake from a lucid dream and hurried out of the store she was in.

Ahead she saw Baxter slipping through the gathered spectators to take up the invisible surveillance baton as the target moved into his zone. He followed the woman into the New-York-style deli at the end of the short block.

Olivia picked up her pace, moving among the transfixed children and parents as if threading a slender needle that only she could see. People stepped aside as she neared, almost as if an unseen magnet repelled them. It was the tracking equivalent of getting a series of green lights along a busy city route.

Olivia refrained from touching her medal, but she sent a wordless prayer of gratitude to whatever power had smoothed her way.

She caught up with the female operative, who'd taken up a position twenty meters ahead of Baxter and now had her cellphone out, speaking into it. Behind the operative was a bakery called Cookie Kitchen, and the scents exuding from it made Olivia remember that she hadn't eaten since breakfast hours before.

She ignored the gurgle in her stomach and walked up to the other CIA officer, who was looking away from her toward the deli.

"Looking for someone?" she asked as the woman turned because her situational awareness had alerted her to Olivia's approach.

The other field officer's jaw dropped.

"Hang up," said Olivia, pleasantly but firmly. "Whoever's on the other end of the line really, really doesn't want a scene in Disneyland. Not to mention all the cameras." She casually waved to the closest security camera along the walk.

The other woman narrowed her eyes and said, "I've been approached by target. Stand by for sitrep." She paused as someone on the other end said something and then answered angrily, "Of course it's Markham! She's fucking standing in front of me, you moron!" She swiped the call button and slipped the phone into her pants pocket.

"You're good, Markham. I had no idea you had someone to use as decoy in Paris. The higher ups are under the impression you didn't know we were coming."

"I don't, and I didn't." Olivia said nothing while the other woman took this in.

She saw when the field officer understood that she and Baxter had been played by chance. It wasn't a good look for the best in the business.

"So, what was so important that you couldn't use your phone to call me?" asked Olivia, letting humor color her voice.

It was also intended to put the other woman off balance following the subtle job critique.

Her colleague shrugged. "No idea. Above my pay grade. All I know is you're considered a serious concern, and we're to follow you and see where you go and who you interact with." Her eyelids flickered at this last part, and Olivia knew she was lying.

She tilted her head, studying the other woman, whose posture signaled that she kept herself on a tight leash. Suddenly Olivia knew who she'd been on the phone with and why.

She laughed. Several nearby people looked at them but turned back to watch the last few vehicles and performers bringing up the end of the afternoon parade.

She gestured to the other operative's pocket. "That was Control telling you where the recovery team waits. And Baxter rarely gets sent on a walk in the park, if you catch my drift." She grinned at her metaphor before sobering.

The other woman scowled. Olivia guessed that she hadn't expected Olivia to call her bluff.

"They're outside the park now. Save yourself and the Company a scene and come with me."

Olivia shook her head, watching the other woman closely. "No. I can't do that. The Agency has been fed malicious intel, but I don't have time or evidence to sort it out."

It was the other CIA officer's turn to laugh. "You really think you can evade being taken by the best recovery expert we've got?"

It was Olivia's turn to shrug. "Maybe not, but I've got to try. Tell Baxter good luck with that reputation of his." She turned on her heel to walk away.

"Tell him yourself." The woman's sharp, triumphant tone shot a warning through Olivia.

She darted a glance toward the deli where Baxter had followed the mistaken target. His intense gaze locked on Olivia's as he made his way toward her.

Crap. The jig was up.

Just then chaos erupted next to him as the 1920s paddy wagon backfired, startling the horses pulling the streetcar, who veered into the crowd on the sidewalk, forcing spectators into a tight clump around the Agency's snatch-and-grab specialist.

Before the female CIA operative could reach Olivia, the last of the costumed performers jostled between them. Olivia spun toward the suddenly empty street behind her and sprinted toward the train station. Beyond it lay the entrance to the theme park. And Baxter's highly trained team.

Olivia raced across the town square, which featured a roundabout where several horse-drawn streetcars and vintage vehicles waited with parkgoers eager to ride down Main Street once the parade cleared. Other visitors to Disneyland scattered as she exited the man-made island that formed the rotary hub, clearing her path to the picturesque station. As she neared the building, which straddled the passage to

Main Street, she tugged the scarf from her head, tucking it into her pants pocket, and slowed down to walk at the back of a group of adolescents who didn't seem to notice.

Somehow, she had to evade skilled operatives trained to take down terrorists, arms dealers, and all-around vicious bad actors.

Capturing a rogue CIA officer would be a piece of cake.

ELEVEN

Olivia made it as far as the train station before she spotted two CIA field officers, who despite casual clothing of polos and chinos, stuck out in the sea of flushed, overly stimulated children and their tired, frowning parents. One had taken point and walked the center aisle of the passage under the station, which was formed by a series of arches and columns, scanning everyone she passed. Twenty meters farther along, her partner brought up the rear, weaving purposefully through the widely spaced columns. Olivia might make it past the first operative, but she'd be unlikely to dodge the second.

She swerved to take the crowded stairs up to the train platform. Above her, several Disney characters stood on a balcony overlooking the town square, waving at passersby.

Olivia looked down toward the people streaming out beneath the train station into the mock town square. The lead female CIA operative came into sight beneath her, apparently unaware that her target had moved up the stairs.

At least until a shout came from across the town square.

Olivia darted a glance over her shoulder to see the CIA officer that she'd confronted outside the Cookie Kitchen hastening through the thick crowds of parkgoers now clogging the area. The woman, focused ahead of her, gestured towards the stairs. The second operative halted and craned her neck as she scanned the people on the stairs. Olivia saw when she recognized her.

Now both operatives began picking their way towards Olivia, who squeezed in front of a large father and managed to make it to the top of the stairs where Snow White stood greeting guests. The third female operative came into view as she did.

"*É!*" said the man. "*Attendez votre tour!*" *Wait your turn!*

Olivia ignored him and brushed past Snow White, who said to the man and his family in an overly sweet voice, "*Allez, revigorez-vous. Ne voulez-vous pas sourire pour moi?*" *Come on, perk up. Won't you smile for me?*

Up ahead, the last passengers boarded the narrow-gauge steam train that took visitors in a large loop around the park. Olivia rushed down the fast-pass lane, where an attendant waved her on. Her good luck held. A single seat remained in the last car with a couple and their three children, the youngest of whom was dressed as a princess. Olivia sat on the same side as the father as the train began to roll slowly out of the station.

The cherubic girl smiled and waved at Olivia before raising her wand and pretending to cast a spell on her. Olivia, tension making her nauseous, did her best to smile at the winsome child. She hoped it didn't resemble a grimace.

Why had the CIA sent a team to bring her in on charges of selling weapons? Even if the evidence seemed damning, their best play would have been to wait until she arrived at the safehouse, none the wiser. What was going on?

As if in answer to her question, her cellphone rang. It was Stasia. Giving the princess's parents an apologetic look, Olivia twisted away as she answered.

"Hey, it's not a good time to talk," she said without preamble. "I'm a bit of a hot potato right now. No need to draw unwanted attention to you and your recent acquisition."

"I am aware. In fact, *cara*, I called to give you some information that you may not have yet. You have been accused of murdering your former asset, Marina Orlova. My friend in the Rome station alerted me that your employer sent a team for you."

Marina had been killed? The news was a gut punch. Shutting her eyes, Olivia curled in on herself and let out a pained breath.

Stasia swore before she could say anything. "I take it that you are dealing with them as we speak? I am so sorry that I could not warn you sooner."

Olivia clenched her teeth to get herself under control. She glanced back at the father next to her, who watched her in open curiosity. "I knew about them, just not why they're here."

"Do you want some help?" The Italian intelligence officer's palpable concern reminded Olivia how alone she truly was.

She sighed. She couldn't drag Stasia into her mess. But for Étienne … she had to grasp at whatever lifeline was thrown at her.

"Not for me," she said, watching the landscape outside the slow-moving train car. They were passing some pine trees bordering a lake. "But my doctor friend will need a travel agent. He's found himself outside of Paris among some unfriendly people."

"What do you need? This number is secure."

Olivia saw what looked like a large, rough-hewn barn from the American Old West. The train, which had never gone faster than a mile or a mile-and-a-half an hour, began to slow. Although she couldn't see inside this station's platform, Olivia knew that someone—or several someones—would be waiting for her.

"I'll call you with details once I'm able to do so. It may be a while. I've got a train to catch."

"Copy that," said Stasia.

Olivia ended the call. She glanced around the train car. The family had gotten embroiled in a conversation about Frontierland, to which the next stop gave access. No one looked at her, except the princess. Olivia smiled at the little girl, who watched her gravely. Placing her forefinger on her lips, she set her cellphone down on the seat next to her and winked.

And then, waving at the little girl, she jumped off the moving railcar, tucking and rolling down the slightly sloping ground into the thick stand of trees.

Stasia looked at her cellphone, frowning and biting her lip after Olivia had ended their call. A sense of foreboding filled her. After a moment, she called the number she had for the Czech military intelligence officer named Andrej Běláček whom she'd met on the unsanctioned operation with Olivia. She made it a habit to collect contacts in other intelligence services, and the young lieutenant had seemed more than willing to go to the top of her list.

"*Ciao, bello,*" she said when he answered. "Have you succeeded in identifying all of the attendees of last year's NATO Days?"

"Not yet, *signorina*. Our investigation has been turned upside down. The Americans claim that they run Bryk as an asset."

"The Americans did not notify your intelligence service of this situation in your backyard?" asked Stasia. Her internal radar had started to tingle. "What about Captain Czerná's investigation into how Bryk acquired the latest Skorpion submachine guns?"

"She has been implicated by the Americans as one of Bryk's sources." Lieutenant Běláček sounded grim. "Of course, that is utter *blbost*. Anyone who has any knowledge of Captain Czerná knows that she would gnaw off her own hand before she would sell weapons of any kind to that *šmejd*, let alone betray her country." He nearly spit the word *scumbag*.

Stasia's radar pinged. First Olivia. And now Beta. She didn't believe in coincidence, especially not when it involved two headstrong women who'd successfully run more than one operation together off the books. *Hanno messo i bastoni tra le ruote a qualcuno.* She'd hazard her vacation pay for the next year that they'd thrown a wrench into someone's works.

She returned her attention to Lieutenant Běláček. "Sources for Czech submachine guns?" Despite her question, she was certain that she knew whom the other "source" implicated was—and who had accused both women.

Lieutenant Běláček's next words confirmed at least the first part of Stasia's theory.

"The story is that Captain Czerná partnered with the American CIA officer Olivia Markham, who traveled to Poland last year to recruit her. Bryk alerted his CIA handler that Markham attempted to purchase a nuclear-detonator package. On his handler's orders, he interfered with the sale."

"Convenient."

"Very." Now Lieutenant Běláček sounded bitter.

"What has happened to Captain Czerná?"

"Someone alerted her to the situation." He paused for a fraction of a second. "She has gone dark. Her handler, Major Vlcek, has ordered me to scour her reports for exculpatory evidence."

"Perhaps the intelligence that Captain Czerná shared with you on the NATO Days will provide you with some."

"It will take time," he said.

"*Ci puoi scommettere!*" said Stasia before translating it into Czech. "You can bet on it. In the meantime, do you have a protocol for contacting Captain Czerná? She may benefit from having a friend in Italian foreign intelligence."

"I am to wait for her to contact me unless it is an emergency." Wariness had replaced the bitterness in Lieutenant Běláček's voice.

"*Certo che sì,*" she said, infusing her own voice with warm agreement. "That is *completely* understandable. And if it were just about clearing her name, I would not suggest it. Tell me, Lieutenant, do you consider Captain Czerná a loyal friend?"

"Yes." He hesitated a moment. "*Per favore,* call me Andrej."

At that Stasia knew that she had him.

"Andrej, I did not get to know Captain Czerná very well on our recent trip to Katowice, but even I could see that she and Olivia Markham have a bond. Signorina Markham needs some emergency tactical support. I intend to give it to her, and I would like to invite Captain Czerná to join me. But I cannot do that without a means to contact her."

"It is because of the American operative that Beta has been forced to go dark!"

"If Captain Czerná is not guilty, I respectfully suggest that neither is Ms. Markham."

Silence reigned for a moment as the Czech officer struggled with dueling loyalties.

And desire to stay in Stasia's good graces.

Finally, Lieutenant Běláček asked, "AISE will be a good friend to Czech intelligence?"

Stasia understood his innuendo.

"*Certo che sì,*" she said again, already planning her next move.

After that, Andrej told Stasia Beta's emergency communication protocol with the dark warning that they were both likely to face the captain's wrath. He did, however, promise to continue digging into the intelligence from the file of unknown provenance with a little guidance from Stasia.

Then Stasia called Major Antonelli.

He answered on the second ring. "Antonelli." His curt voice conveyed a thread of irritation. That was nothing new. He always sounded grumpy post-mission.

"*Su con la vita,* Major," she said. "I have a mission for your team, though I warn you that it must be off the books. It is a favor for me."

"My favorite type of mission," he said, already sounding more cheerful. "No paperwork."

"*Molto bene.* How soon can you be wheels up?" asked Stasia, pressing her success.

"My team has taken a well-deserved leave after Venice. I cannot recall them for simply anything—"

Stasia interrupted him. "Our American friend needs tactical support. Out of country."

"Ah." Major Antonelli sputtered to a pause before continuing. "For our American friend, I will lead an assault team myself."

"I am glad to hear it, *amico mio*. Let us hope that it does not come to that. But we must be pragmatic and plan for the worst. I cannot give you a firm timeframe as of yet, but I believe it will be within the next twenty-four hours. Can I count on your team to be ready?"

Now Major Antonelli bristled. "Have I not said so?"

Olivia never quite knew how she made it out of Disneyland without an epic encounter with Baxter's team. Clearly, they hadn't anticipated her cutting cross country through Frontierland. Even if they had, it was unlikely that they would have sent members after her as she swam across the man-made lake traversed by steamboats and populated with pseudo islands. Despite decades of Hollywood movies showing reckless operators shooting at each other in public settings, the goal of the most effective CIA field officers was to leave little trace of their activities. Which meant doing nothing that would get them arrested. Or on the evening news.

Olivia *did* have to dodge some suspicious Disney "cast members," who spotted her as she walked out of the water near the Phantom Manor. She played dumb, testing what they knew about her, and when the two men threatened to take her to the security office, she begged them to let her go because her husband had a violent temper and would beat her—more—if she embarrassed him.

But she didn't evade all of the CIA operatives in the theme park looking for her.

After winning the sympathies of the two maintenance workers, Olivia managed to reach the plaza between the train station and the Disneyland Hotel at the park entrance. Then she headed for one of the nearby boutiques where she bought the first sweatshirt in her size that she found along with an iconic cap with ears.

It was on the way to the changing room to replace her damp shirt that the Paris tail caught up with Olivia.

The other CIA officer stepped from beside a clothes rack as Olivia walked by, pressing the muzzle of her weapon against Olivia's back and shoving her into the curtained alcove.

"I knew you lied about your decoy," she said.

Olivia didn't stop to question her.

Instead, she pivoted out of the way of the barrel, turning and swinging her right arm up under the other woman's gun arm, trapping the woman's hand against her shoulder. At the same time, Olivia pushed the other CIA officer's extended arm with her left forearm and shoved, hard. The other woman smacked face first against the changing room wall.

Olivia's momentum took her full weight into the other woman's elbow, breaking it. The CIA officer let out a desperate cry of pain. Yet despite the blood gushing down her face, she didn't let the gun go.

So Olivia stepped into her, pinning her injured arm against the wall, and ripped the gun from her limp hand. Then Olivia smashed the butt of the gun into the other woman's head. She dropped to the ground like a sack of potatoes.

"I never lied to a colleague," said Olivia, panting from the exertion. "That's what other operatives do."

She quickly stripped off her damp shirt and pulled the sweatshirt on before shoving the conscripted weapon into the holster she still wore and grabbing the other woman's cellphone. Then she left her "colleague" propped against the bench and went to the lockers where she'd stored her suitcase.

That's where it got weird.

As she pulled her suitcase from the locker, her gaze snagged on a lone woman among the stream of parkgoers returning at the end of the day to retrieve their possessions. It was the same woman from earlier in the day who'd inadvertently distracted the CIA recovery team.

Olivia paused, studying the other woman. She really didn't look that much like Olivia now that Olivia had a chance to observe her. She was slenderer and more delicate, for one thing. Ethereal almost, as if she wasn't from this world. Not like the damp and bruised Olivia, who touched her St. Michael medal at the thought.

After removing her suitcase, the woman locked her luminous blue gaze on Olivia, whom she seemed to recognize.

"'Ello," she said with a Londoner's flair. "Shake off that chap following you?"

Olivia blinked, momentarily bemused.

Before she could speak, the other woman pulled her suitcase closer and lifted a plastic bag with the logo of the New-York-style deli on it. "You appear to need some sustenance. The Reuben sandwich is quite tasty, but the *pain au chocolat* pastries are to die for."

The blonde then handed the bag to the still-speechless Olivia and said, "Cheerio!" as she walked away.

Olivia roused herself to look inside the deli bag to see a wrapped sandwich, several pastries and freshly baked cookies whose scent nearly made her swoon, and another item: a cellphone.

She glanced up as she said, "Hey—you forgot your pho—" only to realize that the British woman was nowhere to be seen.

The sound of the Disney narrow-gauge train coming into the station brought Olivia back to her precarious situation. Tugging her own suitcase from its locker, she hustled toward the Eurostar train station a two-minute walk outside of the park entrance where she bought a ticket for Lille. Although she paid in cash and avoided looking directly at the CCTV, she didn't hide from the security cameras.

However, she changed in the bathroom of the next car over from hers before leaving the Disney sweatshirt, cap, and full suitcase behind. As she stepped off the train, she gave in to temptation and stuffed half a buttery, chocolate-filled pastry into her mouth. Instantly she felt better. The unknown woman was right. They *were* to die for. Olivia sent up a small prayer of gratitude for this unexpected guardian angel and her timely gifts.

From there, Olivia made her careful way to the Paris metro train, making certain that she hadn't picked up any more tails, CIA or otherwise. Once back in the Paris metro area, she recovered her arms cache and go-bag, which had a supply of cash and the Czech passport that she'd had Beta's document forger put together for her the past summer—one the CIA didn't know about. Then she rented a car under the name Emílie Novak.

Twelve hours after evading the CIA recovery team, Olivia checked into a cheap hotel not far from the port in Marseille. The ferry to Tangier Med, the largest port in Africa and, in fact, the entire Mediterranean Sea, left in sixteen hours. She hadn't slept in twenty-four hours.

Before it was time to make her way to the La Méridionale ticket office, she sent Sam a message thanking him for being the best handler and mentor she could have had at the Company.

Then she called Stasia, who answered after the first ring.

"*Fuori di testa per la preoccupazione*," said the diminutive Italian, who despite her words didn't sound at all worried. "My CIA source said you managed to lose the team that was sent after you hours ago."

"Sorry," said Olivia, lying back on the hard hotel bed with its thin comforter. She was suddenly bone tired. "I had some things to gather before I left Paris and a long drive. I wanted to wait until morning to call you anyway." She yawned, covering her mouth to stifle the sound.

Stasia scolded her. "It is not as if I slept, *cara*. Tell me, where is your fiancé and who is holding him?"

"I don't know yet where Étienne is," said Olivia, prevaricating. "As for who has him, it's my good friend Imam Alami."

She had a pretty good idea where Alami had taken Étienne. Stasia had provided enough details of AISE's surveillance on the radical imam during their side operation in Katowice to point Olivia in the right direction. She already knew the rest from the file on his nephew, Hafid. The one who'd blown himself—and her friend Monica—up in Brussels.

"He plans to kill both of you, Olivia," said Stasia.

Olivia laughed. It sounded bitter. "Of course he plans to kill us, but I won't let that happen."

"How? By yourself?" asked Stasia, unbelieving. "Let me give you tactical support."

"When I free Étienne, I need you to get him, Staz, and bring him home safe," said Olivia, swallowing around a rising sob.

She looked across the bed at an open bag on the floor revealing an impressive amount of Semtex and grenades. She'd have more than enough time on the 44-hour ferry ride to develop a tactical plan for rescuing her fiancé.

"If you can stand by for an extraction, I can handle the exchange with this terrorist bastard." She paused. "And if you'd send someone to check on my cat, I'd be eternally grateful."

TWELVE

In reality, Olivia did most of her tactical planning before she even embarked on the ferry.

Even though she didn't have access to Company resources or a tactical team, she'd learned a few things working under the CIA's Assistant Director, who'd assigned her to investigate the Special Activities Division with Sam while she was still a student at the National Intelligence Defense College.

One thing she'd learned: everything can be bought. And so could most people.

From that, she'd deduced that she needed ready access to cash and a line of credit. Or something that functioned like either. Before she left Paris, she'd rented a luxury armored Mercedes modified with hidden compartments to safeguard valuables. In her case, the explosives and ammo that she wanted to bring into Morocco. Whoever waited at the Tanger Med port would "accept" the sedan as a payment for the imam and drive it to Alami's site for her.

She also bought Louis Vuitton luggage, cases of wine and whiskey and another of designer perfume, a harem's worth of lingerie, and a few pornographic magazines. These items would distract the Moroccan customs agents, who would lecture her on avoiding import duties and immorality. The perfume they would let her keep; the rest they would steal. The suitcase filled with tampons, cosmetics, and dirty laundry they would only give a cursory glance, missing her favorite long guns buried beneath them.

Or so she hoped.

After sleeping for a few hours, Olivia rose and went into Marseille to shop for clothing suitable for traveling to an Islamic country. She wouldn't need even a change of underwear once she arrived in Morocco, so she settled on a pair of comfortable leggings and a wide, patterned tunic and shawl. Under the tunic she donned the specially fitted concealed body armor that she'd recovered from her weapons cache. It wouldn't stop rifle fire, but in close combat, it offered some protection against handguns and knives, both of which she carried.

She knew that she'd be searched, so she left a compact Glock 19x in her boots where it would be found and wore a full-size 9mm in a belt holster under her tunic. Then she secreted several tactical knives in places unlikely to be discovered without more intrusive handling: inside her upper thighs, under her armpits along the sides of her torso, and in a special narrow sheath in the valley between her breasts. More intrusive handling was, of course, what Alami intended before he killed Olivia, but she had no intention of letting him use her own knives on her.

Beyond the tactical knives, she wore a pendant with a hidden utility knife and hairpins in her hair. There was a lot she could do with hairpins. Hell, given enough time, she could make Molotov cock-tails from perfume bottles and tampons.

After dressing, Olivia forced herself to eat a hearty meal before loading the Mercedes. She arrived at the ferry line's ticket office at 1900 to pick up the ticket left there for her under the name Amina El Filali.

Alami had a sick sense of humor. Amina El Filali was a 16-year-old woman who'd committed suicide the previous year after being forced to marry her rapist. She'd eaten rat poison out of despair.

At 2000, Olivia drove the reinforced Mercedes onto the ferry and left a set of keys with an attendant. The clock was now ticking on her rendezvous with her nemesis.

Olivia spent the night sleeping as best she could in the cabin that the terror group had booked. She'd trained with the CIA's Special Operations Group, which was populated with hard men who'd done hard things in various U.S. Special Forces groups. They'd taught her that anyone can fall asleep before a high-stakes mission. Even so, her sleep was troubled and short.

Sometime before dawn, Olivia lay on the comfortable bed, twirling her engagement ring on a chain around her neck and re-viewing the Berlin mission.

For a moment, she remembered Thomas, her team leader and lover. After falling for Étienne, she wondered how she could ever have convinced herself that she could be happy with someone so driven, so devoid of tenderness. She'd dodged a bullet when he kicked her off his team.

She shook herself and continued reviewing the intelligence that the CIA had compiled on the terrorist cell, which she'd had a chance to study after bringing Esad to Rome.

During the year that she'd been out of the field, the Agency had tied the two suicide bombers, Hafid Alami and Sadik Bennani, to the Moroccan Islamic Combatant Group, an al-Qaeda affiliate bent on establishing an Islamic Moroccan state that had been active since the early 90s.

Known by its French acronym GICM, the group's membership came primarily from the Moroccan diaspora, with cells throughout Europe. A GICM cell in Belgium was linked to the 2004 Madrid train bombings that killed 191 and injured over 2,000. Despite this, most of the terrorist group's leadership had either been killed or arrested and its members scattered to other al-Qaeda affiliates. But not Imam Alami, whom the Company had only just identified from Esad's interrogation.

A delicate but determined rapping on the cabin door roused Olivia.

Warily, she approached the peephole, her personal Glock 19 in her hands. She could have been knocked over with a feather when she saw who was standing there.

Stasia.

Who stood with her arms crossed and her eyes narrowed.

Olivia opened the door. "What are you doing here?"

Stasia brushed past her smelling of smoky vanilla, like the seductive enchantress she was. That persona evaporated as soon as the Italian super spy turned to confront Olivia.

"Bringing you tactical support." She glared, her hazel gaze snapping as her fingers fluttered around her face. "Although you made it so difficult to find you that I might be forgiven for thinking you planned to go on a suicide mission alone."

"That's because I did," said Olivia. She padded to a chair and sat down, laying the 9 mil on the small desk next to her.

But Stasia wasn't done with her. *"Ma sei proprio un incosciente!"* There was no affection or good humor to soften the Italian idiom. Being called reckless stung a little. "Well, put that thought out of your head, *amica mia*. Of course AISE has a stake in what happens to the terrorist who stole a Predator drone from our country. How dare you not consult us?"

Sheepishness followed by some emotion that Olivia didn't recognize flooded her. "Well, when you put it that way ...."

Stasia came and sat in the cabin's other chair. She fixed a hard stare on Olivia before continuing. "At 0800, we will meet in my cabin for a debriefing with Major Antonelli and your American colleague, who is not so happy with you, Olivia. He wanted me to give you this and remind you about how you came by it."

Stasia set a long black combat knife onto the desk. It was a German KM2000.

Olivia picked the knife up. It had been five years—almost to the day—since she'd wrested it out of the hand of a terrorist on a beach in Ibiza. Her side ached where she'd been stabbed just thinking about it. Only Sam would know that.

Wow. Just wow.

Olivia blinked, trying not to let the tears burning her eyes fall.

"The only thing that would make this even better is if you'd found Beta and recruited her," she said, laughing a little. The words sounded watery and thick.

Stasia crossed her arms. "Beta makes her own way to Morocco. She awaits more details in order to scout sniper locations outside Alami's compound."

Olivia sat, stunned and at a loss for words.

At last, Stasia relented and leaned forward to touch her hand. "Liv, you must know that you have a team with you." Then she sat back. "Now, tell me about your armored car and what you intend to do with it. A Trojan Horse, I presume?"

Olivia grinned at the subtle reminder of their previous mission in Venice. "I'm going to have to change my tactics. You know me too well, *bella*."

When the ferry docked at 1700 on Saturday afternoon at Tanger Med, three bearded men wearing traditional Moroccan garb waited in a Range Rover for Olivia to drive off the ship. They didn't try to hide as they followed her away from the port. They didn't need to. When she'd returned to the Mercedes, she'd found typed instructions waiting for her on the front seat.

She'd been watched on the ferry.

Did Alami know about the Italians? Or Sam?

Cold sweat drenched Olivia's underarms, but she ignored it and the sole customs officer who searched her car afterwards. As predicted, he confiscated the contraband alcohol, lingerie, and pornography. As hoped, he missed the weapons and ammunition hidden inside the specially outfitted Mercedes.

Despite this good fortune, it took Olivia nearly three hours to clear the ferry port. By that time, the tension and heat had merged into a severe headache that threatened to compromise her ability to think, let alone react to her environment.

As instructed, Olivia drove northeast along the coast on the N16 highway. She watched the Range Rover following her, but she saw no sign of her tactical support. After ten minutes, the highway curved south away from the coast. Up ahead, Olivia recognized the restaurant where her instructions had told her to stop.

She pulled into the lot, her escort trailing closely behind. Thirty seconds later a tall, unsmiling *jihadi* yanked the driver's-side door open and ordered her out. After a quick search in which he took her two handguns, her new bodyguard bound her wrists behind her back and dropped a black bag over her head. Despite anticipating everything that was happening to her, Olivia's heart tapped like a frantic hummingbird at her rib cage.

Her captor shoved her into the backseat of the Mercedes before driving away. For a moment, Olivia felt totally disoriented. Then she felt the St. Michael medal against the skin of her chest. Taking a slow breath, she focused on what she could discern even with the stifling fabric of the bag limiting her senses.

Though dark, some daylight still managed to seep through the weave of the fabric covering her face. Olivia knew that they continued east on the highway. So far, their route fit her guesswork about Alami's base of operations, which placed it not far from the Strait of Gibraltar and easy access to Europe.

She'd noted Alami's Arabic dialect when she first encountered him in Berlin. It had been unusual enough that Olivia spent some time working up a profile on the terrorist while Reardon kept her busy on graymail during her time at the Prague station. Although he spoke *Darija*, the dialect of Arabic spoken in Morocco that included many words borrowed from Berber, French, and Spanish, Olivia had heard the Spanish influence in Alami's speech. Because Spain still controlled two cities on the Mediterranean coast, Ceuta and Melilla, she'd further refined the target area within the northern Rif region.

If she had to guess—and, frankly, she did—from all of the activity that both the CIA and AISE had tied to the GICM remnant in Morocco, Olivia would choose the port of Al Hoceima, the small capital of the province of the same name, as the site of Alami's lair.

But the nearby and larger city of Nador also had an international airport and a history of smuggling cheap goods from Spain and China. Alami, like most terrorists, funded many of his operations via smuggling. Yet a large terrorist cell with links to GICM and AQIM had been arrested in Al Hoceima only half a dozen years ago.

If she'd guessed wrong, she might pay with her life ... and Étienne's.

It was after midnight when they finally stopped. Olivia's mouth was as dry as cotton and her shoulders ached even though she'd tried to lift and rotate them. The driver got out as the passenger door next to her opened.

The familiar scent of the Moroccan cooking spice *ras el hanout* wafted over Olivia, filled with pungent notes of coriander, cardamon, black pepper, allspice, paprika and at least half a dozen other spices that Olivia didn't have time to name.

Then someone yanked her from the car by her upper arm.

Someone else prodded her in the small of her back, and Olivia stumbled forward in the dark, the viselike grip still on her arm. Mottled light diffused the darkness inside her head covering. Once her sense of smell had adjusted, the mineral scent of the ocean mixed with the warm scent of asphalt under her feet. From the sounds of their steps bouncing from hard surfaces nearby, Olivia knew that they walked down a narrow street lined with cars.

Soon she would be with Étienne.

Her escort guided her roughly through a narrow doorway and up a short flight of uneven stairs. Olivia stubbed her toes on a riser and went down on her knees, hard, before being pulled to her feet and ordered to continue. At the top of the stairs, she was shoved through another doorway, and then the bag was tugged from her head.

For a moment, Olivia blinked in the incandescent light of a small living room, dragging in air after hours of shallow breathing. Dizziness washed over her. With effort she straightened, pulled her shoulders down, and lifted her chin until her vision focused.

Then bit her tongue until she tasted blood at what she saw.

Étienne sat slumped on a stool, completely naked, bruised, and bloody with his hands chained together to the wall above his head. At first, Olivia feared that he was dead, but then she noted the slight rise and fall of his chest. Next to him stood Merjam's husband Zouhair, his gaze venomous and hot, his hands bloody.

When Olivia winced, a man behind her laughed. "I will enjoy delivering Allah's justice to you, demon."

Alami. He planned to watch her being humiliated.

In the periphery of her vision, she saw her driver and another *jihadi* standing on either side of the room. They each held automatic rifles against their chests and watched her with hard gazes.

"Of course, you remember Zouhair," said the terrorist leader, who sat on a large cushion on the floor in the nearly empty room. His malevolent gaze and acid tone sent chills through her. "He begged for permission to take from you what you took from him."

Olivia swallowed, trying to moisten her dry throat. She had to keep Alami talking as long as she could. She turned to face her interlocuter. When she spoke, her words came out as a hoarse whisper. "Merjam asked for help. She wasn't tortured."

Alami studied her. Then he nodded to Zouhair, who stepped forward and struck Olivia with his closed fist. Jagged pain exploded inside her skull like a fragmentation grenade. She collapsed to her knees like a sack of potatoes, toppling onto her side, and vomited.

"Not only are you a *kafir* who disbelieves in the truth of Islam, you're an agent of American intelligence working against Allah's believers. You have no authority over Merjam."

Olivia struggled to rise to her knees. She spat the vomit clinging to her lips away and glared at Zouhair who raised his fist.

She glanced at the terrorist leader. "What about her brother Esad?"

Alami held his hand up to restrain Zouhair, who'd growled and grabbed Olivia's shoulder to pull her to her feet.

"Speak," he said to Olivia.

"Esad didn't know that you forced Merjam to marry Zouhair, whom he hates," said Olivia, ignoring the threatening man gripping her. "As the head of his family, he wouldn't have given his permission. We didn't have to torture him, either, to get him to tell us about your plans. We just let him reunite with his sister."

Zouhair's fingers tightened just before he struck her again. Olivia's knees buckled. She didn't know how long she could sustain this beating, but a quick glance at Étienne shot steel down her spine. She could keep it up long enough to keep her fiancé from being hurt any more.

Alami's eyes narrowed. "Then it was a poor trade. Esad knew very little about our plans. He was simply a delivery driver."

Now Olivia cocked her head, affecting a casualness that she really didn't feel. "I wouldn't say that. His intel led the Italians to the Predator drone you stole from them."

Alami's dark gaze flashed as he stood. He stepped closer to Olivia, his hand reaching for her chin to hold it in a vise-like grip. He was so close that she smelled the tobacco clinging to him and saw the large pores in his cheeks.

She held his gaze defiantly, ready for a blow, but instead he turned to one of the men standing guard. "Go! Check with our brothers to see if she tells the truth."

The man nodded and left the room.

Good. Now there were only three *jihadis* with Étienne and her.

Olivia felt the KM2000 in its sheath along her spine. Her fingers could reach its handle at the small of her back. But she ignored its temptation to focus on Alami.

"It's the truth. I was there when they recovered it. In fact," she said, leaning closer, "I'm the one who told them where to find it. A boathouse in Venice under their noses all this time? Very clever. Too bad you won't be able to use it in Turkey against LANDCOM."

Alami's eyes widened, confirming that Olivia had guessed his target. "How did you discover this?" he demanded.

Étienne moaned. It took all of Olivia's willpower not to dart a look at him. Her St. Michael medal grew heavy against her chest, inspiring her next words.

Narrowing her eyes, she leaned in and said in a low voice, "I'm not a demon, but an angel. How else can I shock and awe?"

At the code phrase, the night outside exploded, shaking the building. Brilliant light lit the room. The acrid scent of explosives wrestled with the shrieks of car alarms and a myriad shouting voices. The three terrorists tumbled to the floor as glass shattered into the room.

Olivia, her feet planted in anticipation of Stasia detonating the Mercedes outside, recovered first. She tugged with numb fingers at the blade of the KM2000, sliding it down a few centimeters before sawing at the flexible cord binding her wrists.

Alami, Zouhair, and the third *jihadi* struggled to their feet. Étienne's stool had shifted under him so that he'd fallen to his knees with his arms stretched above his head, completely awake.

As she worked, she willed Étienne to look at her. She couldn't risk drawing the *jihadis'* attention to him, not now, not when they were so close to freedom. But she wanted to convey that she was right where she wanted to be. That she had a plan to save him.

By some miracle, Étienne sensed her gaze and looked at her.

Please, please let him trust in me. Her medal warmed.

Out on the street, automatic gunfire ripped through the chaotic noise. Olivia recognized the sounds of the HK416 assault rifle that Major Antonelli's commandos used. The AK47s of Alami's men chattered in response.

Fury swept across Alami's features. "Kill her!"

The *jihadi* lifted his rifle.

Only to collapse as an unseen sniper took him out.

Beta.

Zouhair, growling, lunged for Olivia, whose wrists were still bound. Abandoning the combat knife, she rolled away from him. Across from them, Alami bent and wrenched the discarded rifle out of the dead man's hands. Warning shrieked through Olivia. Alami wasn't in front of the window. And then Zouhair loomed over her. Olivia brought her knees into her chest and kicked, hard. Zouhair staggered back.

Alami stood and aimed at Olivia. But nothing happened when he pulled the trigger. He looked incredulous. The AK had miraculously jammed.

Zouhair came at Olivia again.

She bucked and kept her legs tucked against her chest as he tried to pry them apart, still struggling to slice through her wrist restraint. They moved around the small space, knocking into the stool and forcing Alami to dodge their writhing figures. Olivia was dimly aware that the terrorist leader sought to unjam the weapon he held by clearing the chamber.

Olivia kicked her heel into Zouhair's face, stunning him. But he was far from unconscious. and her hands and wrists had gotten cut on the razor edge of the combat knife as they wrestled, slicking her fingers with hot blood.

As Zouhair came at Olivia again, she gave up on the KM2000. Instead, she opened her legs, wrapping one behind his neck and pulling him forward. He fell against her with a loud exhale, and then her second leg completed the triangle choke. Locking her ankles, she bridged her back and squeezed her thighs before twisting, hard, and snapping his neck. Then she got her heels onto the dead man's shoulders and kicked him from her.

"Blasphemous ape!" shouted Alami.

She looked up in time to see the terrorist leader throw the malfunctioning magazine away. He bent to remove a magazine from the dead *jihadi*'s ammo belt.

Olivia rolled to the side and renewed her effort to slice through the rope. Just as the blade slipped through the cord enough that she could break the remaining fibers with a concerted pull, Alami stood. He slammed the fresh magazine into the well on the Russian-made automatic rifle.

Their gazes locked.

All at once, Olivia knew what he intended. She sprang to her feet.

Several things happened simultaneously.

Screaming "No!" Olivia leapt at Alami as he raised the assault rifle toward Étienne.

Feet sounded on the stairs outside.

The AK spat bullets as Olivia knocked its barrel up and plowed into Alami, who staggered backward but remained upright.

Then Stasia appeared in the doorway as Olivia grabbed the rifle and tried to wrench it from Alami. The terrorist leader let go with a hand to reach around to Olivia's back where the KM2000 remained halfway inserted in its sheath.

He tugged it free and stabbed it toward Olivia's side …

… only to stiffen as Stasia shot him through the temple.

And Beta shot him through the rear of his skull, sending brain matter and blood in an explosive mist that rained down on everyone in the room.

For a brief instant all motion stopped as if caught in a freeze frame, Olivia's vision crystal clear in a way that told her just how alive she was—and how close she'd come to dying.

And then Alami collapsed, taking Olivia to the floor where her own blood from the bullets that had pierced her spread in an expanding pool beneath her.

Darkness rushed to swallow Olivia. Before she lost consciousness, she saw Sam Ahren in the door to the room, smoke and dust begriming his face and tactical clothing. In his hands, he held an M14. Their gazes caught. She saw relief and irritation in his, but all she felt was gratitude.

"Markham, when are you going to wait for me before you take out red zebs?" he asked, referring to the name his SOG team had given enemy Islamic combatants—and the first time he'd found her on the beach at Ibiza. "I'm tired of seeing you bleed."

THIRTEEN

Olivia woke some time later in a hospital bed. Her right shoulder burned and ached so fiercely it made her vision swim. She swallowed hard and looked down at the thick bandage visible under the neckline of her gown. Another fiery ache in her abdomen made her breath catch on an inhale. Clenching her jaws, she pulled the covering blanket and sheet aside and peered down her torso but could only make out the lumpy outline of sterile dressing.

The door to her hospital room opened and a nurse peeked in. Seeing that Olivia was awake, she came in and checked Olivia's vitals before going to the window and opening the blinds.

"You have a visitor, *fraulein*," said the nurse in German as she turned back to Olivia.

Olivia nodded but said nothing. She had a feeling that she had a series of visitors in her immediate future, a thought which exhausted her already.

The nurse came and helped her to sit upright against the raised hospital bed before handing her a plastic cup with a straw. Then she left. Dizziness washed over Olivia, but she closed her eyes and focused on breathing until the vertigo passed.

When she raised them, shock filled her at what she saw. Sam held the door open with one foot as he pushed a wheelchair with Étienne inside her room.

Emotion flooded Olivia along with tears thickening her throat. She hadn't realized until she saw Étienne how terror had anchored in her soul at not knowing whether he'd been killed.

Sam guided the wheelchair closer to Olivia's hospital bed, then locked the brake.

He looked at both of them, his usual good humor quiescent. "I think you two have some catching up to do. More than you can manage in this setting, but I can already tell that Markham needed to see you, Dr. Dumond."

After he'd addressed Étienne, Sam looked at Olivia. "We can have a high-level after-action review later, Markham. Suffice it to say, it's a doozy, even for you."

She nodded dumbly and watched as he left her alone with her fiancé. It felt like he'd left her alone with a tribunal set to judge her for dereliction of duty.

Étienne's hollow cheeks and eyes made him look haunted. He had a deep laceration along one cheekbone that left an ugly purple bruise like a bulls' eye against his gray-tinged skin. His chapped lips and bandaged hands competed with the deep raspberry of burns along his throat. Olivia's memory of him, naked and chained to the wall, filled in the rest of the injuries hidden under Étienne's hospital gown.

Silence dragged out between them until Olivia dropped her gaze and picked at the blanket covering her.

Finally, Étienne cleared his throat. "I spoke to your surgeon. He says that both bullets caused less damage than he anticipated. In fact, you are healing exceptionally well. Even your eye where that odious man struck you is no longer swollen and red. You will be released in a few days." He paused, then continued in what sounded like forced casualness. "I spoke to my landlady. You will be relieved to hear that she has been caring for Cleo, who has grown quite fat, I am certain."

Olivia looked up at Étienne. Tears threatened again. "I'll never forgive myself for what happened to you," she whispered.

Something flitted across his face. Then he said, "You saved Merjam and her baby, *oui*?"

Olivia nodded and brushed a tear away.

"Then you and I are alike, *ma cherie*. We both do what we can to help others."

A small sob escaped Olivia at Étienne's generosity. "I will always love you, Étienne," she said, her voice shaking, "but you're a healer who fights against death. Sometimes I have to deal it to save others."

"Including me."

"Including you."

She sucked in a breath, steadying herself. Étienne said nothing, simply watched her. She knew that he knew what was coming. It was one of his gifts as a pediatric oncologist, this empathy and understanding for his young patients.

She would have liked to see him as a father.

"I want you to understand that I really intended to marry you and leave fieldwork," she said, slowly and carefully, holding his gaze with her own.

Pain knifed her. This hurt more than being shot twice.

He nodded. "I know."

She took another deep breath. "But I belong in the field." She clutched the blanket over her, suddenly desperate for Étienne to understand. "I–I don't know how to explain this ... it just feels like what I've been called to do. Like it's a mission from God."

A weighty silence fell between them.

At last Étienne said what Olivia had yet to bring herself to say. "And you do not believe that you are called to marry me."

"I don't think I'm called to marry anyone."

Étienne surprised Olivia then by leaning forward and laying a bandaged hand on her thigh. "No," he said with conviction, "I refuse to believe that, *ma cherie*. You are worthy of love. Moreover, the world will be a better place when your children are in it. It is simply a matter of when God will bring the right man into your life."

"I wanted it to be you," she said.

Étienne's gaze searched hers. Then he sat back. "Whoever he is, he will be a lion among men, *ma cherie*. A man whose mission complements yours, not supersedes it."

"Are you sure he exists?" asked Olivia, doubt and hope warring in her. "He sounds almost mythological." She laughed now.

"*Non,*" said Étienne, shaking his head, "he might be as rare as you are, but he's real. Of that I have no doubt. God would not leave you alone in your mission."

Later, after Sam had returned and wheeled Étienne back to his room, Olivia sat morose and silent, unable to sleep and replaying her conversation with her former fiancé. The nurse had been surprised when Olivia insisted that she take out the morphine drip, but she didn't want to be in a fog anymore. Besides, she'd learned over the previous five years that her tolerance to pain was higher than average.

A few hours after that, the door to her hospital room opened again. This time, Stasia held a tray with Olivia's lunch. Behind her, Beta peered over the petite Italian, her dark gaze unfathomable.

Stasia smiled warmly as she brought the tray to Olivia, Beta trailing behind. "I brought you some food, *cara*."

She adjusted the folding table on Olivia's hospital bed and set the tray down. It held a plate of what looked like *cacio e pepe*, the Italian spaghetti dish with Romano and Parmesan cheese. Next to it were green beans, bread, and the creamy *panna cotta* pudding.

"Of course, it is not sanctioned, so please do not inform on me, I beg you." She winked.

Olivia, who hadn't realized how hungry she was until she smelled the delicious food, making her stomach growl, reached for a spoon and fork. "Why would you ever think I'd tell the powers that be that you snuck contraband food into me? I would only be hurting myself."

She swirled some of the pasta onto her fork against the bowl of the spoon, slipped the laden utensil into her mouth, and sighed noisily as she tasted the simple, yet hearty dish. She forced herself to chew slowly, savoring the *al dente* pasta.

Stasia, looking quite pleased, sat in the bedside chair while Beta leaned against the wall behind her. "I am relieved that you like my cooking, Liv. It has been so long since I cooked a meal that I feared that I might have to give up my Italian citizenship."

Olivia swallowed. "The only thing that would make this better is a glass of *falanghina*," she said, referring to a light white wine drunk in the Campania region.

Now Stasia's eyes practically lit up, the green tones in the hazel brightening. "Your wish is my command," she said, producing a bottle from the oversized purse hanging from her shoulder.

Olivia laughed. "I will never doubt your skills as an intelligence operative again."

Stasia arched a brow. "Did you ever?"

Olivia laughed again, shaking her head. "No, not really."

Olivia continued eating while Stasia handed the bottle to Beta along with a bottle opener. Then she pulled out three plastic stemless wineglasses. After Stasia poured them each some wine, Beta took hers and stood guard by the door.

When Olivia had finished her lunch, including the decadent dessert smothered in limoncello, she sighed and sat back.

"*Grazie mille, amica mio.* I feel almost human again. "

Stasia smiled. "You will be out in the field again before you know it."

Olivia looked away as she reached for her wineglass. This was the whole crux of the matter, the reason she'd just ended her engagement to the man she loved.

Yet she didn't really know how she could continue in the field.

Stasia seemed to read her mind. "Do not fear, *bella*. All will work out, I predict. Your colleague, Sam Ahren, moved heaven and earth to come to your aid in Morocco. He can fill you in all of the details regarding the murder investigation of your former asset. However, he has read me in on the most important part, that is, that you are no longer suspected of killing her."

Olivia's gaze flew to Stasia, who watched her gravely. "How? I was working with you and Beta when she got killed. I don't have an alibi, not one I can share with my employer anyway."

Stasia tilted her head. "Why not? You were working with Italian intelligence on a joint operation against the GICM remnant cell led by Alami. A successful operation, I might add. I wrote the report myself."

Olivia's eyes widened. "But I was a Company housekeeper in transition to a new assignment, not an active field officer."

Stasia pressed her lips together and shrugged, her upraised hands eloquent. "That is not what your handler, Sam Ahren, told the CIA when he brought you to this Company site in Germany."

"Okay," said Olivia, bemused at this turn of events. It explained the absence of armed guards and why she wasn't handcuffed to the hospital bed. "I can't wait for Sam to tell me what he found out in Prague. Someone was handling Marina off the books. I bet if he found that person, he'd find her killer."

Now Beta spoke from her position next to the door. "That is no mystery. It is your previous station chief, James Reardon."

Olivia had suspected this all along but hadn't want to voice her suspicions without any evidence. "But why?"

"Likely because she discovered that Reardon and Bryk were in bed together," said Stasia.

"What?" Now Olivia was just dumbfounded.

Beta answered. "They met at last year's Czech-sponsored NATO days. It was in the intelligence file left at our interrogation site. The one that is still unsourced."

Stasia, glancing at Beta, who nodded, continued. "AISE uncovered Savik's connections last year after the Venice raid. I was focused on tracking the buyer of the Predator, but I tasked some of my colleagues to continue cataloguing everyone with whom the Serb had done business. There was a mysterious supplier, one who needed to move next generation Skorpions."

"Reardon?" asked Olivia, still in shock. Reardon had always seemed like a straight arrow. A little officious and pedantic, sure. But not someone who would be a traitor. A murderous traitor.

Beta took up the story now. "After I brought Bryk in, someone from the CIA claimed to have run him as an asset for the past year. According to Bryk, you recruited me last year when you came to Katowice to buy the nuclear-detonator package."

"A sale that I learned about from my Russian asset." Olivia's shock had faded, and her brain pieced the last of the puzzle together. "Making me a traitor and motivating me to kill Marina."

Stasia nodded. Beta just stared at Olivia with an intensity that would have given her chills if she hadn't known the Czech better.

"I suppose that you informed the CIA of your findings?"

Stasia shook her head. "No, Sam Ahren did."

"Ah." Olivia thought for a moment. "As part of the joint operation with AISE, he uncovered Reardon's illicit activities. He probably has the receipts, now, too."

"*Senza dubbio, cara.*" Stasia grinned. She left it unsaid that she'd supplied most of them.

Olivia looked at Beta. "I'm relieved on your behalf, Beta. I wouldn't forgive myself if you were out in the cold because of me."

Beta shrugged a shoulder. "Why? You are not responsible for what a traitor in your agency does. It is all part of the game, Liv. My handler knows me. He would have cleared my name eventually." She sniffed. "I am too valuable for my country to let the CIA dictate my future."

Olivia nodded. "Well, I'm glad that your name was cleared sooner rather than later, nonetheless." She sighed, and then looked at each of her friends as she spoke. "By the way, thank you both for coming to my rescue." She swallowed and continued. "Étienne and I wouldn't have survived without you."

Beta raised an eyebrow and said nothing.

Stasia rolled her eyes. "It was the right thing to do."

Olivia should have felt relieved that she had a future in the CIA after everything was said and done. Instead, disquiet filled her.

She would be returning to the field. Why did she feel so empty?

She looked up. Both Beta and Stasia watched her with something like expectation.

After a moment, realization dawned on Olivia.

"You two didn't need to tell me all of this in person. Together," she added. "Our unsanctioned operation has come to an end." She looked at each of them. "Unless I'm missing something."

Stasia glanced at Beta, whose slight chin nod signaled her agreement. The interaction amazed Olivia, who would have expected the other two operatives to be at odds.

"We would like to continue our work together, Olivia." She leaned forward in her chair to hold Olivia's gaze. "You have pushed us to do something more than stop bombs and bullets. We want to use our skills and resources to help innocent people, not just target bad guys."

"We are a very effective team," said Beta. "I do not come to that conclusion lightly."

"I know," said Olivia, astounded. And something else.

Excited. And hopeful.

Blinking to clear her suddenly misty vision, she said, "Well, then, I propose that we continue our unsanctioned collaboration, our guardian initiative, for as long as we can."

Six weeks later, Olivia had returned to Kotor and the Ladder. It was late August, and she had just a few more days before she was expected to report to the Vienna substation, her next field assignment. She'd already visited Lejla and Ayman to give them news of Merjam and her brother and to check on Nika, whose care had been transferred to a new pediatric oncologist. She'd brought the little girl a gift: Cleo, who deserved a loving mistress who would never abandon him. She had one more task before conquering the Ladder, but its prospect no longer weighed on her.

Her shoulder was still a little stiff, and her side ached if she pushed too much, but she'd decided that it didn't matter how long it took her to scale the entire length of the Ladder. She'd take however long it took—all day if need be—to reach the top and Cetinje.

As she climbed wearing the foot gloves that her father had given her, Olivia recalled her recent visit home. Her parents, to her dismay, had gotten older in her absence. Her father had more gray in his hair, and his cheeks had started to lengthen into jowls. His hairline had even receded, and his hair had thinned. Her mother, who'd always been trim, had gained some weight around her middle and worry lines around her mouth. Neither of Olivia's younger siblings had been home, having graduated college and moved.

It made Olivia sad, yet more determined than ever to spend her life doing something meaningful.

Sam had returned to meet Olivia at the same CIA facility where she'd been transported after being stabbed five years before.

She thought about that visit as she reached the Chapel of St. John, where the metal gate barring entrance inexplicably stood ajar.

"You know, Markham, it wasn't all me," he said, his gray eyes serious. "Some help came from the most unlikely places. Take the Company snatch-and-grab guy, for example."

"Baxter?" she asked.

He nodded. "He found a file you left behind at the Kotor safehouse. He spent a lot of time poring over it. He didn't believe anyone who'd done the work you did on your own could be the traitor that Reardon claimed. He brought the file to me. That's how I found your AISE contact. And the rest is history as they say."

He also told her how Julia had put the nail in Reardon's coffin with a detailed accounting of his years' long abuse of the Prague station finances, and the financial threads she'd found from this audit, one that had been overlooked by other CIA auditors. Even now, Olivia's old teammate worked on the case the CIA brought against its former employee and the trove of intelligence on Central and Eastern European criminal networks that had been uncovered as a result.

Sam had told her plainly that she could continue her side activities because he believed in her and would do his best to help her if she needed it.

As she left Étienne's engagement ring inside the medieval chapel, Olivia thought about the strange coincidences and fortuitous events that had kept her on her path, rocky and indirect though it had been, like this improbable Ladder up the mountainside. Despite the twists and turns—and the summit still unseen—she'd always moved steadily upward.

It was almost as if she had divine help, if she believed in that sort of thing. And it was as much as any human could ask for.

 Liane Zane is the cover identity of a novelist who is an expert at hiding in plain sight. She has spent time interrogating a former Army intelligence officer and engaging in Open-Source Intelligence (OSINT) activities related to Italian slang words for naughty body parts and the proclivities of Eastern European criminals. She spends her days drinking New England chocolate-raspberry coffee and gazing at the magical brook in her back yard as she plots her romantic thrillers or walking her dogs along mountain trails near her estate-like home.

THE GUARDIAN INITIATIVE (Book Three) is the third book in Liane's series, THE UNSANCTIONED GUARDIANS, which narrates the genesis of the Wild *Elioud* (Olivia, Beta, and Stasia) first introduced in THE *ELIOUD* LEGACY into a disciplined team of covert advocates for innocent victims, especially of sex trafficking and assault. THE COVERT GUARDIAN (Book One) and THE HAR-LEQUIN PROTOCOL (Book Two) complete the prequel trilogy.

THE *ELIOUD* LEGACY comprises THE HARLEQUIN & THE DRANGÙE (Olivia & Mihàil's story), THE FLOWER & THE

BLACKBIRD (Stasia & Miró's story), and THE DRAKA & THE GIANT (Beta and András's story). All three books tell the complex legacy of the *Elioud* descendants of the Fallen Watcher Angels and are therefore best read in order.

Visit www.lianezane.com for updates and to buy merchandise related to the series.

ALSO BY LIANE ZANE

The Elioud Legacy
The Harlequin & The Drangùe
The Flower & The Blackbird
The Draka & The Giant

The Unsanctioned Guardians
(prequel to The *Elioud* Legacy)
The Covert Guardian
The Harlequin Protocol
The Guardian Initiative

Available in paperback, ebook, and audiobook online at www.liane zane.com as well as all major retailers or through your local library by request. Check the copyright page for the ISBN numbers to expedite ordering.